"Is it so hard to imagine that you and I have something in common?" Andrew asked, turning to face Sadie.

"No, I guess not." Sadie paused on her porch and drew in deep breaths of the cool, fall air, perfumed with the scent. Tilting her face to the sun, she said, "It's just that you and I live our lives so differently."

"Do we?" He held his hand out for her to take. "I think we live our lives very much the same—all or nothing. I've seen you with your students and you throw yourself completely into it."

The warmth of his fingers on hers was like the rays of the sun. She savored the feel, realizing sometime that day she had given up the notion they were just friends. It was more than that, at least on her part, and that thought scared her.

D0951797

Books by Margaret Daley

Love Inspired

The Power of Love #168
Family for Keeps #183
Sadie's Hero #191

MARGARET DALEY

feels she has been blessed. She has been married thirty-one years to her husband, Mike, whom she met in college. He is a terrific support and her best friend. They have one son, Shaun, who is marrying his high school sweetheart.

Margaret has been writing for many years and loves to tell a story. When she was a little girl, she would play with her dolls and make up stories about their lives. Now she writes these stories down. She especially enjoys weaving stories about families and how faith in God can sustain a person when things get tough. When she isn't writing, she is fortunate to be a teacher for students with special needs. She has taught for over twenty years and loves working with her students. She has also been a Special Olympics coach and participated in many sports with her students.

Sadie's Hero
Margaret Daley

Published by Steeple Hill Books™

STEEPLE HILL BOOKS

Steeple
Hill™

ISBN 0-373-87198-8

SADIE'S HERO

Visit us at www.steeplehill.com

Printed in U.S.A.

Though he fall, he shall not be utterly cast down:
for the Lord upholdeth him with his hand.
—*Psalms* 37:24

I want to dedicate this book
to the people who work with Special Olympics
in Oklahoma and to a special coach, Laurie.

Chapter One

Bachelor number forty-six: Andrew Knight, 37, is a senior vice president of International Foods. When not working, he likes to play golf and read. With black hair and gray eyes he is any woman's idea of a dream date, especially the one he plans, dinner at Maison Blanche followed by a concert on the lawn of Philbrook Museum of Art in Tulsa.

Sadie Spencer read the description in the catalog, then looked at the man who was number forty-six. He stood on the platform in a black tuxedo that fit him perfectly. Made for him, she decided as her gaze traveled up his tall length to rest on his face, sculpted in clean, strong lines. She had to agree with the catalog's description. He did inspire dreams.

"The opening bid for our next bachelor offered on

the auction block tonight is two hundred dollars. Do I hear two twenty-five?''

"Two hundred twenty-five," a distinguished-looking woman in the front row shouted.

"I thought you wanted to bid on him," Carol West whispered to Sadie.

Her friend's urgent words focused Sadie on her mission. "Four hundred dollars."

Everyone turned toward Sadie, and for a few seconds silence reigned in the hotel banquet room. Leaning against the back wall, she shifted from one foot to the other, her throat suddenly very dry. The room seemed unusually hot.

"Sadie, are you crazy? I don't know why I even bother asking. Of course, you are." Carol's astonishment, mixed with her exasperation, was evident in her round eyes and furrowed brow.

"It's for a good cause—fifteen good causes, in fact," Sadie whispered, never taking her gaze off number forty-six. "I've got to have him."

"Four hundred fifty," the distinguished-looking woman countered, shooting Sadie a look of determination.

"Five hundred," she returned, mentally calculating how much she could bid and still have enough for the next month's rent. She really hadn't thought the bid would go so high, but she wasn't going to give in when she was so close to her goal.

"Five twenty-five."

Sadie turned to Carol. "Will you loan me fifty? I've been trying for two months to get past his secretary. I'm a desperate woman. This plan has divine inspiration—well, not exactly divine, but when I saw his name on the list of bachelors for this auction, I knew my prayers had been answered. I know this will work. Please, Carol.''

With a deep sigh her friend nodded.

"Five hundred fifty," Sadie said, aware all eyes were on her, including Andrew Knight's. His cool regard trapped her, momentarily wiping all reason from her mind. She tried to ignore the tingling sensation that streaked up her spine but she couldn't. Sweat broke out on her upper lip. She resisted the urge to wipe away the sign of her nervousness while *he* watched.

Determinedly she pulled her gaze from him. With a willpower she was beginning to think she'd lost, Sadie fixed her attention on the woman in the front row and silently pleaded for her to give up. She held her breath while waiting for the woman to bid again. If she did, Sadie would be forced to come up with another way to meet Andrew Knight. When the woman shook her head, Sadie relaxed her tensed shoulders.

"Five fifty once." The auctioneer's visual sweep of the room seemed minutes long rather than seconds. "Twice." Another pause, Sadie was sure for dramatic effect. "Sold to the lady in red for five hundred fifty dollars."

"I realize the man is gorgeous, but it isn't too late to back out." Carol's frown was deeply in place.

"His looks are beside the point. You know why I

need to meet with him. His company is perfect for what I have in mind." Sadie still felt his intense, piercing gray gaze on her and found herself drawn to the platform.

"There are less expensive ways to see Andrew Knight. I'm sure with your vivid imagination you'd have come up with a way to get past his barracuda secretary. You always do think of something in time."

Carol's words barely registered in Sadie's mind. Instead, she felt ensnared by assessing eyes and couldn't look away from the man her friend was discussing. Much to Sadie's dismay, she had the impression of being probed, cataloged and filed away in a matter of a few seconds by Mr. Andrew Knight. With a blush flaming her face, she averted her gaze, resolved not to look again. Apparently her vivid imagination was working overtime this evening.

"Carol, school will be over before I get in to see him if I don't do something fast. I've tried to get past that woman who guards his door as if her life depends on it. And perhaps it does."

"You're much too melodramatic for your own good. Life indeed!"

"I don't mean her life literally, but I do mean her job. It's his eyes and the way he carries himself." Sadie gestured toward the stage but didn't dare look at the man. "There's something about him that's so intense—almost brooding." *Or perhaps it's ruthless determination,* she concluded silently, not sure from where that impression came.

"You need an outlet for that imagination of yours. Have you ever thought about writing?"

"No," Sadie answered immediately, her smile vanishing.

"It's got to be in your genes," her friend continued as if Sadie hadn't said anything. "Your father's historical characterizations are great. He makes those people seem so alive and real. That last book he wrote about Napoleon was fascinating."

The air became stuffy, Sadie's chest tight with each breath. Standing in the back of the room with the other organizers of the annual fund-raiser, she took the opportunity to slip out the door into the hallway. As she inhaled deeply, Carol joined her.

"Are you all right, Sadie? You're so pale."

She waved her hand in the air, dismissing her friend's concern. "Too many people in there. Our turnout was much larger this year."

"Since you're on the board of Children Charities, you're in the position to get a larger room for the auction next year. Have you decided what you're going to say to Mr. Knight?"

"Me? Plan ahead? Only when absolutely necessary."

"In other words, you haven't the slightest idea how you're going to sell him on the work project."

"Of course, I know. I'm going to appeal to his soft vulnerable side, to his love of children. If I can convince IFI to go along with my project, then the other companies in the area will follow like cattle to the slaughter."

"From what I've heard there may not be a soft, vulnerable side to appeal to. I suppose he might love children, but he has been a confirmed bachelor for thirty-seven years."

"The first twenty don't count. Too young to marry. Something will come to me when I'm having dinner with him. If not, by the time he takes me to the concert, I should have come up with the right approach."

Carol's laughter rang in the silent hallway. "If anyone can come up with the perfect approach, it'll be you. Come on. We'd better get back inside. It sounds like the auction is over."

Perfect. The word stuck in Sadie's mind as she walked back into the room. All her life she had striven to be perfect because that was what her father had demanded. When she had brought home an A minus on her report card, her father had wanted an A. When she had brought home an A, he had wanted an A plus. She had always come up short in his eyes, never quite the daughter he wanted. Thankfully she had found salvation in the Lord. As a teenager, lost, hurting, she had turned to her church's youth group for solace when her father had been particularly tough on her self-esteem. Now she couldn't imagine her life without the Lord's guidance.

"I'd better pay for this date or I won't be going anywhere." Sadie made her way to the table at the side set up for that purpose.

"I see you won our number forty-six." Jollie Randall took Sadie's check. "You know, I was the one to recruit him for this auction. Most reluctant, though. Wanted to donate money instead. Don't scare him off, Sadie. We could use him next year.''

"He could get married.''

"Not likely. I work at IFI, and there have been many women who have tried to snare him, but he doesn't have the time for a serious relationship.''

Good, Sadie thought. She didn't want a commitment, just his okay on her work project. "Then he's safe for next year.

"I'll send Mr. Andrew Knight back in one piece and you can save your money for next year's auction.''

Jollie's eyes widened, and her mouth fell open.

Sadie felt pinpricks go up her spine. She slowly turned. Her whole face reddened as she stared into the subject of their conversation's unreadable gray eyes.

"As soon as you two ladies finish planning my future, I'd like a word with you.'' Andrew directed his comment to Sadie.

Intense might be too mild a word to describe Andrew Knight, Sadie thought as she continued to stare at him, her mind blank of any response to give him. She was sure her face rivaled her red dress.

His eyes warmed to a dove gray. "About the arrangements, Miss—''

"Sadie Spencer.''

"Miss Spencer.'' He extended his hand.

When his fingers closed around hers, she wasn't surprised at the firm handshake that transmitted confidence and determination nor the warmth that spread up her arm at the tactile contact. For a few seconds she felt surrounded by him, a taut pressure building in her chest. Then he released her hand, and the tension eased, allowing her to breathe again.

"About the arrangements, Mr. Knight. May I have a word with you in private?" There was nothing she could do about the quaver in her voice, which signified the disruption this man caused to her equilibrium. She glanced about the room full of people, all talking at once. "I think there's a small room off this one we can use."

"Lead the way, Miss Spencer."

"Please call me Sadie. Only my students call me Miss Spencer."

He started walking beside her toward the room she had indicated. "You're a teacher?"

"At Cimarron High School. I teach students with special needs."

"That must be very demanding work that requires a lot of patience." Andrew opened the door for Sadie.

"My job is demanding, like a lot of people's, but I love working with my students. They're what make my job rewarding," Sadie said as she entered the room.

"I'm afraid I haven't been around any children with special needs. In fact, I haven't been around many children." Andrew shut the door, enclosing them in the suddenly small space.

Even though a few feet separated them, Sadie felt overwhelmed by his presence. He filled the room with his intensity. He leaned against a table and crossed his arms. An amused look softened his stern features as several minutes passed and Sadie remained silent, trying to figure out the best way to approach him about her work project. Nothing came to mind except the fact that he'd said he hadn't been around people with special needs. She needed to change that before approaching him about working with them, or his answer would probably be no even before she had presented the whole work project to him.

"Sadie." He finally broke into the quiet. "You said you wanted to speak with me in private. Since the hour is growing late and tomorrow is a workday—"

"But it's Sunday." *The Lord's day.*

He arched his brow and quirked his mouth. "Some people do work on Sunday. I get more work done on Sunday when everyone else is gone than I do two days during the week."

"Well, then." Sadie began to pace, nervous energy compelling her to move. "I have to confess I had a reason for bidding on you tonight." She stopped and faced him, deciding only to tell him about part of her plan. "I want IFI to help support Cimarron High School's Special Olympics program. Since you're the vice president of special projects and human resources, I thought you would be the person to see at IFI. For example, at the school we're in desperate need of uniforms."

"Why didn't you take the five hundred fifty dollars you spent on this date and buy uniforms with it?"

"Because we need continual support, not a one-time shot in the arm. New uniforms will have to be purchased every year as our program grows. Fees to the state games in May paid every year. Some equipment purchased.''

"I see. Wouldn't it have been easier to contact me at my office?'' His facade of cool businessman descended over his features.

"I tried, but your secretary said you've been too busy to see anyone right now. Something about being out of town a lot lately on business. So when this opportunity came up, I decided to bypass normal channels.''

He raised one eyebrow. "Have you always been unorthodox?''

Sadie laughed. "I have been accused of that a few times. Since I give to Children Charities every year, I thought it was a brilliant plan.''

"IFI is constantly being approached about donating to good causes. Sometimes Mrs. Fox screens the requests and the people seeking appointments not connected directly with IFI, especially when I'm particularly busy at work.''

"Then you weren't out of town?''

"No, I was. Since you went to so much trouble, I'll take a look at your proposal. Write up what you need in the way of support and get it to me as soon as possible. I'll have an answer for you by the time we go on our date. I assume you still want to go?''

Sadie nodded, aware of the polite distance he was putting between them.

Glancing at his watch, he straightened away from

the table. "Would next Saturday night be okay? I have tickets for the concert for that night."

"Yes, that would be fine."

"I'll call you about the time closer to the day."

His tone of voice conveyed their conversation was over. As Sadie walked toward the door, she wasn't sure just how she was going to get him involved when he was so busy. Between now and their date she would have to come up with an offer the man couldn't refuse.

Andrew sat behind his massive desk in his office, staring out the window. The morning so far had been unproductive. He usually enjoyed these quiet times the most, but today he was restless, reflective. He rarely thought about his past because he felt it was a waste of time, something he didn't allow himself to do. But this morning he had to fight the memories he worked so hard to suppress.

No! He wouldn't permit his past to intrude now. He needed to turn around and concentrate on the Madison project. But he had one of those dreams last night, and afterward he always had a difficult time not giving in to his emotions.

At thirty-seven he was one of the four senior vice presidents of a large international food corporation. Most of his special projects he'd worked on involved enhancing IFI's reputation in the community and marketplace. His hard work the past fifteen years had paid off. He should be elated, on top of the world. He wasn't. Lately he had felt more and more a vague restlessness, as though something was missing from his life, and when he did, he didn't feel in control. He wouldn't tolerate that.

A knock startled him from his reflection. He swiveled his chair to face the door. "Come in."

Bill, one of the guards on duty downstairs, came into the office, followed by Sadie Spencer. "Mr. Knight, she says she has an appointment with you. I told her you don't meet with people on Sundays. I started to send her away, but she persuaded me to check with you first. She said you're expecting some kind of proposal from her." Bill lowered his gaze to the carpet. "I didn't want to turn her away if that was true."

Andrew contained his smile at the sheepish look on the guard's face. After his brief encounter with Sadie Spencer the night before, Andrew could just imagine her unusual kind of persuasion. "Thanks, Bill. I'll take care of Miss Spencer."

"I hope you and Frank enjoy my chocolate doughnuts," Sadie said as the guard left.

Andrew chuckled. "So that's how you got the man to bring you up here. Bill and Frank usually guard my privacy like a mother hen guarding the chicken coop. I'm going to have to speak with them about women bearing gifts of food."

Sadie crossed the room, sat in front of his desk and placed several pieces of paper, a box and a thermos with two mugs before him. "I hope you aren't too angry with them. After all, you told me to get my proposal about Special Olympics to you as soon as possible. I stayed up last night so you could have it first thing this morning before I go to church.''

"I'm impressed." He glanced at his watch. "It's only nine, less than twelve hours since I saw you last. I wish I could get my employees to work that fast." He picked up the papers and flipped through them. "You did all this last night after the banquet?"

"Yes. It's important."

He lifted his gaze from the proposal, locking with hers across his desktop. Her brown hair was pulled back in a French braid. Her face, with her pleasing features, held only a touch of makeup. She looked refreshed, ready to take on the world. But it was her eyes that drew him. They were dark, almost black. For a fleeting moment while they stared at each other, he sensed a haunting vulnerability she tried to conceal from the world. But he knew it was there beneath the surface and wondered what or who was responsible for putting it there. He felt a connection to her that momentarily stunned him.

He cleared his throat and looked away, dismissing the common bond. "I'll get back with you concerning your proposal as soon as I've studied it." His gaze fell to the box. "You said chocolate doughnuts? I must confess I have a weakness for chocolate."

"Chocolate has that effect on people. I, too, love it, but I also have oat bran muffins with me. I don't want to be accused of feeding you only unhealthy food. I baked these this morning." She opened the box and began to withdraw all the goodies she brought.

Andrew watched, fascinated. Not only were there doughnuts and oat bran muffins, but also a coffee cake and cinnamon rolls. "You baked all these this morning!"

"Well—" she paused and peered at him "—after finishing the proposal at three, I couldn't go to sleep, so I baked. I like to cook. I find it soothing."

He watched her as she walked across his office and wondered where in the world she put all the food she cooked. There wasn't an ounce of fat on her. She had all the right curves for her small frame. "What do you do with the food you cook?"

"I eat it. That or I invite some friends over to help me." She closed the box and put it on the floor next to her chair. "Or I freeze it. Of course, I have to have a party periodically to clean out my freezer."

Her voice was tinged with laughter, and he felt himself responding to that. It was a rich sound that was comforting. It touched his restlessness and soothed him.

"Would you like some coffee?" Sadie asked, holding up the thermos. "I'd better warn you there's something a little extra in my coffee."

Before he could answer, she started pouring two mugs full. He eyed the coffee as she handed it to him. "Something extra?"

"I have several secret blends. This is what I call my morning pick-me-upper."

Andrew cautiously brought the mug to his lips, taking a deep breath of the wonderful aroma, and sipped. The coffee slid down his throat, warming him all the way. It was strong but smooth with no bitter after-taste. "This is delicious. What's in it?"

She smiled, a smile that made her dark eyes sparkle like polished jet that caught in the sunshine. "A woman has to have some secrets. I'm usually an open book except for some of my special recipes." The smile deepened, bringing a playfully wicked gleam to her eyes. "I figured you would be ready for breakfast about now."

"How did you know I didn't have breakfast this morning?"

"Just a guess, but I bet food is unimportant to you."

"Why do you say that? We have to have food to exist." Andrew bit into a rich doughnut with melted chocolate dripping off it.

"I saw you eating last night at the banquet, and you hardly noticed the food you were putting into your mouth. You think of food as a way to keep yourself alive. I think of food as a delicious experience to be relished."

He began to chew the doughnut more slowly, taking notice of its sweet taste for the first time. He had never thought about his eating habits, but he supposed he did rush through his meals, rarely taking notice of what he ate, as Sadie Spencer pointed out after only one observation. Suddenly he was disconcerted that someone was able to read him so well in such a short time. He had worked hard not to reveal himself to others.

"I bet you usually skip breakfast, too." Sadie interrupted his thoughts. "If you have anything it's probably a cup of coffee when you get to work."

"Have you been following me?" He picked up an oat bran muffin and began eating it while she refilled his mug.

"No, but I've known many people just like you. Most have their biggest meal at night, when for weight purposes it should be either at breakfast or lunch. Breakfast is when I eat the most. That way I have all day to work off the calories." She stopped talking abruptly. "Excuse me. I have a habit of going on and on at times. It's the teacher in me. I teach nutrition and cooking to my students and can't resist talking about the subject. Just hold up a hand when you want me to stop. Breakfast is a great way—"

With his hand raised, he chuckled. Sadie Spencer was just what he needed to forget his melancholy mood. She swept into his office with mouthwatering temptations and a bright smile that dazzled a person. He was glad she had come, and he couldn't believe he wasn't upset that someone had interrupted him on a Sunday, which just wasn't done.

"You've sold me on the fact that breakfast is important." Andrew held up the cinnamon roll he was going to sample. "You're certainly more than a teacher."

"Why, of course. Everyone is more than what they do for a living. I'm sure in your spare time you do a lot of things. It just so happens that I love to cook in my spare time." Tilting her head to the side, she smiled again. "Well, one of the things I like to do."

"What are some of the other things you like to do?"

"Besides teaching, which I love, I'm involved in Special Olympics and Children Charities, but you already know that. I am also a Sunday school teacher—six- and seven-year-olds. I like to read anything having to do with history, and I do the usual sporting things, tennis, golf, swimming, skiing—"

"Whoa." Andrew raised his hand again. "When do you rest? I thought I was busy, but you're wearing me out listening to all your activities."

"Oh, what kind of hobbies do you have?" She snapped her fingers. "No, wait. The catalog said you like to play golf and read. So we do have something in common. What do you like to read?"

He frowned, trying to remember the last book he had read for pleasure. "Tons of stuff, all related to work. And before you ask about golf, when I do play it is for business purposes."

"Those aren't hobbies."

"I don't have much spare time."

"You work all the time?"

He straightened in his chair, his frown growing more pronounced. "I enjoy working."

She started to pour some more coffee, but he shook his head. "So do I, but I also enjoy my free time, too. All work makes—"

"Don't say it." Her teasing censure made him feel uncomfortable, as though he had wasted half his life climbing the corporate ladder. Andrew shifted the papers on his desk, then continued in a businesslike voice. "And speaking of work, I have a lot still to do today, and didn't you say something about going to church?" He didn't usually have to defend his work habits with the people he knew, and he didn't want to start now. His job had served him well over the years.

"Yes, but..." For a second, surprise flickered in her dark eyes. Quickly she lowered her lashes and busied herself cleaning up.

Andrew watched as she put everything into the box and closed the lid. He would consider her proposal, take her out on the date she'd paid for, and that would be all. It would end as quickly as it had begun. Relationships were always so much easier when they were kept on a friendly but impersonal basis. He had learned that painfully when he had been shuffled from one foster family to the next.

Sadie scooted the box toward him, then rose. "I've left you some food for later." She extended her hand across the desk, no expression in her expressive eyes now. "Thank you for taking the time to look at my proposal."

Her tone equaled his in stiff politeness. Rising, he accepted her hand, needing this meeting to come to an end as soon as possible. "I'll call you about the date later in the week."

After picking up her thermos and mugs, she started to say something, but instead just stared at him. The darkness of her eyes intensified as a small frown knitted her brows. Andrew knew she was debating whether to speak her mind. He was surprised when she decided not to and turned to leave. His curiosity was aroused as he watched her walk toward the door. What had she wanted to say to him, and why hadn't she? He was sure she usually spoke her mind. She was probably not afraid of many people.

The sound of the door clicking shut reverberated through the office, and for a few seconds he felt totally alone, as though no one else existed in the world. A tight band about his chest tautened, constricting his breathing. Why did he feel as though he'd let Sadie Spencer down? And why did he care?

Chapter Two

Sadie couldn't quite believe she was traveling to the Crescent City to have her date with Andrew Knight. That morning he'd called her from New Orleans, where a business negotiation had lasted longer than he'd thought it would. He would have to stay the whole day. He'd left it up to her—to come in IFI's jet, which was bringing a sales team to a conference or to wait until some indefinite time in the future for their date. She'd told him immediately that she would come to New Orleans, because she didn't know when the man would ever have the time to fit her into his work-consuming schedule. She wanted to get him involved with her students, but how was she going to accomplish that between all his business meetings?

Sadie was jolted from her musings when the stewardess announced the jet was preparing to land at New Orleans International Airport. She checked to make sure her seat belt was fastened, then tried to ready herself mentally for the landing, her hands gripping the arms of the chair so tightly her knuckles were white. She certainly wasn't destined to be a world traveler. She was fine in the air, but the takeoffs and landings always reminded her of how fragile life was and that at this moment she wasn't at all in control of it.

"Dear Lord, please give me the strength to persuade this man to give my students a chance at working in the community. Guide me and help me see Your path. In Jesus's name, amen," she murmured, the prayer taking her mind off the plane's descent.

When the jet touched ground, Sadie inhaled, then exhaled a deep breath. She tried not to think that she still had the return flight to get through. At least she wouldn't be alone and would be able to talk to Andrew to take her mind off flying.

As she descended the steps from the jet, she was accosted by the stifling heat of an October afternoon in New Orleans. The humidity blanketed her in a fine sheen, and she remembered all the time that morning she had taken to apply her makeup and to select the right sundress to wear. Ruined after one minute, she thought with a silent laugh.

At the bottom of the steps she scanned the area. No Andrew Knight. As she was trying to decide what to do, a white limousine approached the jet, and a chauffeur climbed out of the car.

"Miss Spencer?"

"Yes?"

"Mr. Knight sent me to pick you up. He regretted

yet another delay, but by the time you arrive at the house, he will be through with his business.''

''Where's Mr. Knight?'' Sadie asked, puzzled about where his meeting was taking place.

''At Oakcrest Plantation. My employer owns the plantation. It's outside New Orleans. About a thirty-minute drive, Miss Spencer.''

''Is your employer Mr. Madison?'' Andrew had mentioned the man on the phone that morning. The negotiations must be taking place at his house.

''Yes, ma'am.''

The chauffeur opened the back door for her, and she slid into the luxurious car, the soft feel of leather beneath her fingertips. On the ride out of New Orleans, she savored the distinctive sights of the river city. She particularly loved its history with its French and Spanish heritage. She should return one day and really see the city and its Southern culture. The romantic, as well as the historian, in her demanded it.

The gray shadows of dusk spread across the landscape as the limousine pulled into a long driveway lined with huge oaks that formed a canopy over the lane. Spanish moss dripped from their branches as though the trees were weeping. She felt like she was suddenly back in the time right before the Civil War and was going to a weekend ball at a neighboring plantation.

She was beginning to visualize herself dressed in a hoop skirt made of yards and yards of silk material when the car stopped in front of the massive front veranda. Sadie looked out the window at the eight tall columns and white facade and fell in love with the place. She wished she had a home like this. Such a romantic, she chided herself and climbed out of the car when the chauffeur opened the back door.

Andrew came onto the veranda. The beautiful house behind him was eclipsed by his presence. Pausing on the steps, Sadie allowed her gaze to trek up his length, her earlier impression of his single-minded ruthlessness reconfirmed. What arrested her about Andrew Knight was the sense this man before her was tough, aggressive, individualistic, a man who controlled his own destiny. He would stand out in a room crowded with successful men. His regard held an intensity of purpose she seldom encountered.

"I'm sorry I couldn't make it to the airport, Sadie. I trust your flight was okay?"

"Yes," she murmured, suddenly not sure how to act. She was inundated with the feeling she shouldn't be here, that she was starting something that could hurt her in the end.

"Darrell and I just finished twenty minutes ago."

Sadie was surprised to find Andrew dressed casually in black slacks and a white polo shirt. She had expected no less than a three-piece business suit, since he had been working. In her brief encounters with him he'd seemed like a man who followed business protocol down to the last stitch of clothing. But then, if she thought about her presence in New Orleans, she would have to admit that her being here was a bit unusual in itself. She couldn't see him mixing business with pleasure. He was definitely a complex man, full of contradictions, she decided.

"Let's go inside, and I'll introduce you to Darrell and his wife."

Andrew motioned for her to go first, resting his hand at the small of her back. It wasn't an intimate gesture but a casual one. Even knowing that, Sadie couldn't help the quickening of her heartbeat as she entered the antebellum home.

Inside the foyer he dropped his hand. "They're in the den at the back of the house. Ruth and Darrell Madison, besides being good friends, don't stand on ceremony. They insisted I ask you to join us and were glad you decided to."

"Are we dining here tonight?"

"Yes. Mabel, their cook, is one of the best. I think you'll enjoy her creations."

"Only if we have a truly Cajun meal," she said with a laugh. "Otherwise—" She turned at the den door to stare at Andrew and forgot what she was going to say.

His clean scent, spicing the air, made her aware of his presence only inches from her. His handsome features erased everything from her mind but him and her together in a dim hallway.

"Otherwise what?" Amusement laced his voice while his gray eyes shimmered with laughter.

"Otherwise I might just have to insist on you taking me to Antoine's tonight."

"Without reservations on a Saturday night?"

"Don't you know somebody with pull?"

"Afraid not."

Sadie exaggerated a pout. "And all the way down here I couldn't get Cajun food out of my mind. I swear the minute I landed I thought I smelled seafood gumbo."

His chuckle slid over her as though they had been friends for years. "You're in luck. Mabel loves to impress guests with her Cajun cooking."

"I knew this would be my lucky day. One of my wishes has come true."

"One of them?" A thick brow rose as his smile crinkled the corners of his eyes. "That implies there's more than one. What is your other wish?"

Sadie had to step back. He overpowered her. "Now, if I told you, none of the others would come true," she replied, a breathless quality entering her voice, the distance between them still too close.

"Others! My, you're ambitious."

"I prefer the word hopeful."

He leaned nearer, reaching around her to grasp the doorknob. "When I return you to Cimarron City, I'd be interested in how I did with the others."

"Are you sure you want to know?" She was struggling to think straight with him so close. Her mind kept dwelling on his arm, which was brushing hers, his eyes, which were like molten silver as they looked at her, his mouth, which formed a half smile that was melting her insides.

"That sounds ominous. Exactly how many wishes are we talking about?"

"Only two others."

He turned the knob and pushed the door open. "That doesn't sound too overwhelming. I think I can handle that. I've got big shoulders."

Sadie entered the den first, followed by Andrew, who quickly made the introductions. Sadie shook Ruth's and Darrell's hands, immediately liking them. Their den reflected the couple, cozy, friendly, warm, the fragrance of fresh flowers filling the air from several arrangements on tables about the room.

"Andrew told us a little about this bachelor auction but not nearly enough to satisfy my curiosity," Ruth said as they all sat. "What a neat idea for raising money. How long has your organization been doing it?"

"Four years."

"It sounds like a dating game," Darrell said, scooting closer to his wife on the couch.

"It's all done in fun and for charity, but there have been several marriages that have come from the couples meeting at the auction. That might be why our turnout every year grows. We started with twenty bachelors, and this year we auctioned off fifty. The number of women attending has doubled just in the last year."

"I must confess when he told me I couldn't picture him agreeing. How in the world did you ever talk Andrew into being one?" Ruth slipped her hand into her husband's.

"I didn't. Someone at IFI did, and from what I heard it wasn't easy. You might compare it to moving Mount Rushmore."

Andrew held up his hand. "Hold it. I have to say in my defense that I know how hectic my schedule can be. I didn't want there to be any problems."

Darrell's laugh was deep and hearty. "Like today. He drives a hard bargain, especially when he's under pressure to get the negotiations over with."

"I should also add in his defense he tried to buy off the woman who asked him by donating some money to the charity in his place. He just doesn't know how valuable a real live bachelor is."

"Now that sounds like the Andrew I know," Ruth said. "The true businessman to the letter. His time is much too valuable for something as trivial as a date."

Andrew bent close to Sadie and whispered loud enough for the couple across from them to hear, "Forget that I said Darrell and Ruth were friends."

Sadie hoped for once her face wouldn't flame. Andrew's nearness sent a shiver coursing through her. Her heartbeat and breathing were quickly becoming erratic. She added a fourth wish to her list; she wanted to know what one of his kisses felt like.

"Don't let Andrew fool you, Sadie. Darrell and he have been friends since high school. In fact, I guess we all three have been." Ruth rose, squeezed her husband's hand, released it, then said to Sadie, "Let's leave the men alone for a while. I want to show you the house. You should have seen it when Darrell and I bought it eight years ago. What a mess! I'm proud of what we've done to preserve a little history. I'll let Andrew show you the gardens and gazebo later."

* * *

Andrew watched Sadie leave the room, surprised at how glad he was she'd taken him up on his invitation to dine in New Orleans. Silence, thick and heavy like the humidity outside, fell between Darrell and him as the door clicked shut.

Andrew stood and walked to the mantel. "You can quit staring at me like that now."

"Like what?" Darrell exaggerated an innocent look.

"Like you're waiting for a confession. There's nothing to tell. I hardly know Sadie. She bid on me at the auction last weekend, and that was the first time I met her." Andrew recalled how she'd breezed into his office the following day and had nearly taken over in a short space of time.

"And you brought her here to New Orleans?"

"Is that supposed to mean something?"

"No." Darrell answered slowly, paused for a long moment, then asked, "Does she know you grew up not far from this house?"

Andrew stared at the empty grate in the fireplace. "That's not important. Irrelevant to the moment at hand."

"Is it?"

Andrew's head shot up and his gaze clashed with his friend's. "I'll have the contracts to you by the end of the week."

"Okay. As usual the past is off-limits. I just find it interesting that you brought a woman here. That's a first."

"When I make an appointment, I like to keep it."

"Business ones, yes, but ones for pleasure I doubt have that kind of devotion."

"In a way this is business between Sadie and me." Andrew kneaded the cords of his neck, feeling the tension beneath his hand. That was the only way he would consider the unorthodox invitation.

"Business? Is this how you're justifying this unusual move to yourself?"

Seated again on the couch, Andrew leaned forward, his elbows on his knees, his hands clasped loosely together. "Why do you want to read more into this than there is?"

Darrell shrugged. "Chalk it up to a friend who cares what happens to you. I've followed you through the years. I've watched you try to shake your past. I've seen you work incessantly up the corporate ladder. But I've witnessed the longing on your face when you visit here. There's a void in your life, and you don't quite know how to fix it."

"I'm fulfilling an obligation to take Sadie Spencer out. She paid for the date. That sounds like a business arrangement to me." When Andrew looked into his friend's face and saw the skepticism in his expression, he added, "Yes, I think she's an interesting woman."

"Just interesting? Have you gone blind since we last met?"

Andrew visualized Sadie. Her shoulder-length brown hair framed an oval face that was striking, with its satin-like skin, high cheekbones, full lips and dark intense eyes that could put a man in a trance. "Okay. She's beautiful, too. But that is all, Darrell. This date is as far as my relationship with her will go. I have too much still to do to complicate my life right now.''

''The presidency of IFI?''

''Yes. Lawrence Wilson will retire in a year. I want the job.''

''Along with several other vice presidents. It won't be an easy fight. The prize is a big one, if that's what you want.''

''Yes, it's what I want,'' Andrew said, aware his voice held a defensive tone in it, which he knew Darrell heard, too. ''Have I ever turned my back on a hard fight? The tougher the better.''

''So you'll put your personal life on hold. You've been doing that for fifteen years. When will you take time for yourself?''

''Next year.''

''You remember Gregory Hansom?''

''A year ahead of us in school?''

''Yes. He had a heart attack last week. Nearly died. The doctor told him if he didn't change his lifestyle and reduce his stress the next one would finish him for good. Is that what you want?''

''It's not going to happen to me. I exercise when I can and eat right.'' Andrew winced inwardly when he remembered how often he skipped breakfast and the fact that Sadie had called him on that.

''How often do you exercise?''

''Have we gone back in time to the Spanish Inquisition?''

''How often?''

''I try to get to the health club once a week.''

"And do you make it?"

"Sometimes." Andrew rose, restless energy demanding a release. "I wonder what's keeping the women." He started for the door.

"You don't have to escape. I'll drop the questions. You're a big boy now and have to live your own life."

Andrew turned at the door, a forced smile on his face. "Thanks. Now I'll sleep better at night."

"Come on back over here and tell me what's going on at IFI. Let the women have some time to get to know each other."

The darkness caressed Sadie with its cool fingers. As she leaned into the lacework railing of the gazebo, she inhaled the jasmine-laden air with hints of honeysuckle woven in it. Listening to the night sounds, she cleared her mind of all her troubles and relished the moment for what it was—a small, peaceful heartbeat in time when everything was right with the world. A gift from God.

Andrew came to stand next to her. "I like to come out here when I'm visiting. Ruth loves her gardens. She spends a lot of time working in them."

"I love a beautiful garden, too, but I'm afraid I don't have what it takes to be a gardener."

"Oh, what?"

"A green thumb." She held out her fist with her thumb sticking up. "Definitely black. I even killed a cactus once by under-watering it. But that character flaw doesn't stop me from appreciating a heavenly place, and this garden and gazebo are.''

''Darrell built this for Ruth as a surprise when she was in the hospital having their daughter.''

''How romantic,'' Sadie said, closing her eyes to hold the image of herself next to an attractive, intelligent man who captured more than she dared to allow.

''I suppose it was. Darrell and Ruth often do little and big things like that for each other. Even when they were dating in high school.''

Sadie heard the envious tone in Andrew's voice and felt a kinship with him. All through dinner with the couple and their seven-year-old daughter, Sadie had sensed a deep caring and love expressed in their respect for each other. They had taken time for each other, never demanding, never criticizing. Carrie, their daughter, was lucky she didn't have to live up to her parents' expectations of her. As Sadie knew from experience, that was difficult on a child. It left emotional wounds that were hard to heal.

''How long have they been married?'' Sadie finally asked, realizing Andrew was staring at her, producing a tightening in her chest.

''Nineteen years.''

''Nineteen!'' Sadie pushed away from the railing, stepping back to face Andrew as he turned toward her. ''They act like newlyweds.''

His low, warm chuckle erased all other sounds and made everything so much more intimate. ''Sadie, some people do stay married, even though I must admit it's not as common as it once was.''

She tried to read his expression, but the dark shadows hid it. ''You sound like a cynic. Have you ever been married?''

''Do you always speak your mind?''

''Yes. Have you?''

''No. How about yourself?''

She shook her head.

''I thought a die-hard romantic like you, Sadie, would have been by now.''

''It's because I am that I've never married.''

''Now who sounds like the cynic?''

She shrugged. ''Darrell and Ruth are lucky. I've seen so many couples who aren't. Marriage is for a lifetime. I've just found that the dreams are usually better than the real thing.''

''Then there are no disappointments?''

''Right.''

''But you can't hold dreams.''

Sadie shifted away from Andrew. She didn't like the way the conversation was developing. Carol had told her that very same thing several times in the past year. She knew she had many friends but no one she wanted to get close to for the kind of relationship necessary for a marriage to work. ''A relationship has its ups and downs, but that's what makes it exciting.'' Carol's words came back to Sadie. *But when you open yourself up to another, they see all your flaws.*

''I thought you were a die-hard workaholic,'' she said, trailing her hand along the wooden railing as she distanced herself some more. "When do you have time to squeeze in a relationship?"

His laughter blanketed the night like the cloak of darkness. "I deserved that. I don't, any more than you do. For different reasons we have something in common." Lounging against the railing, he folded his arms across his chest. "Actually, those were Darrell's words. He keeps hounding me to slow down and smell the roses."

"I think Darrell's right. Take a deep breath."

"What?"

"Really. Smell Ruth's roses. They smell wonderful." As she listened to Andrew inhale, she was drawn toward him until mere inches separated them. "When you came out here before, did you ever just enjoy the atmosphere, the flowers, the quiet?"

"Well, no. I like to come out here to think. It's a good place to work through a problem I might be having at IFI. Darrell has accused me of only visiting them to do just that."

"Sometimes it's nice to stop and savor a place for what it is. To wipe your mind clean of all thoughts and relish the moment of peace. I find that helps relieve my stress more than anything else."

"Attacking problems head-on works best for me."

"But I bet you're always at war, fighting something. Don't you ever get tired of it all?"

Andrew didn't answer for a long moment. When he did, his voice was stiff. "If you want something, you have to fight for it. The world isn't going to give you a thing."

His cold words reminded Sadie of why she was here in the first place. She knew the value of fighting for what she wanted. "Have you made a decision about my proposal concerning Special Olympics?" she asked in a no-nonsense voice.

"Yes, we'll be able to do what you requested."

"Oh, fantastic!" Sadie paused, took a deep breath, then said, "I have another favor to ask. Will you come Thursday night to the high school for a meeting and reception with the parents and students involved in Special Olympics? As IFI's representative you could formally give us the money at the meeting."

"I don't—"

"It would be good PR for IFI," she interjected, her stomach twisted with tension.

"What time?"

"Seven, in the high school auditorium."

"I'll be there."

"Thanks," she whispered, sensing his sharp gaze on her as though he were trying to discern what was beneath her request.

She could come to care a great deal for this man beside her. He possessed a certain vulnerability that matched hers and pulled her to him, body and soul. Their outlooks on life were light-years apart. She doubted he went to church, if last Sunday at the office was any indication. Her faith was what sustained her. His work was what sustained him, she suspected, and yet she felt a common bond she couldn't deny.

Chapter Three

"What are you not telling me, Sadie?"

Andrew's question cut into Sadie's thoughts and set alarm bells ringing in her mind. It was too soon to approach him about her work project. He was sharp, intuitive, no doubt two qualities that served him well in the business world. She couldn't let down her guard for a second around him. He endangered her peace of mind more than anyone had in a long time. This had to be kept purely professional—a working relationship, she vowed, as she placed some distance between them and faced him.

"Andrew Knight, it's just a simple request to meet my students. That's all." She pressed her lips together to emphasize her point and hoped he didn't pursue his question. She wasn't ready to tell him the main reason she had bid on him. She wanted him to see how capable her students were.

He started to say something when he heard his

name being called from the house. "We'd better head back."

At the French doors that led into the living room, Ruth intercepted them. "Andrew, there's a call for you. You can take it in the den."

While he went to answer the phone, Sadie remained with Ruth, thankful for the timely interruption. "Your gardens are beautiful. I wish I could have seen more, but we need to leave soon."

"You're welcome at my home any time. Maybe you can persuade Andrew to bring you down again. Maybe even get him to take some time off. He works way too much."

Sadie knew the instant he reappeared even though she didn't see him come into the living room. Her body tightened with awareness as if every part of her were attuned to him. She glanced toward him and saw the frown that knitted his brow. "What's wrong?"

"That was the IFI pilot. He has to leave immediately for New York. He won't be able to take us back to Cimarron City tonight, like I had planned. We can either take a commercial flight or wait until he can pick us up tomorrow evening."

"Well, then it's settled," Ruth said. "Now y'all will be able to see more of Oakcrest. Y'all can stay here tonight."

Indecision clouded Andrew's eyes. He started to speak.

"Andrew, I won't take no for an answer. Sadie can use some of my clothes. What do you think?" Ruth turned to Sadie.

She looked from the woman to Andrew. "It'll be okay with me. I don't have anything planned special for tomorrow. I can call a friend to teach my Sunday school class."

"Great. You can go with us to church tomorrow. I've been wanting to get Andrew to our little church, and this will be a perfect time to visit. I'll go get your bedrooms ready." Ruth hurried into the foyer as though afraid if she didn't rush Andrew would decline to stay the night.

The living room suddenly seemed small as Sadie faced him, not sure what he was thinking. His features had flattened into a neutral expression while his body was still tense. The silence between them stretched, marred only by the ticking of the grandfather clock. The rhythmic sound echoed in her mind, grating against her taut nerves.

"I'd forgotten how important Sundays at the office are to you. If you want to get a commercial flight, that's fine by me." Sadie welcomed the sound of her voice. It cut through the tension.

Andrew glanced at the grandfather clock in the corner. "It's too late. I've already tried."

Disappointment speared through her chest, leaving a dull ache in her heart. "Did you get reservations for tomorrow morning?"

"No. I had some things I needed to do, but by the time we got home the day would be half over."

"So you decided to take a day off?"

He nodded. "I haven't had one in several months."

"You have been busy. No wonder Mrs. Fox is so protective of you."

"We work well together. She's as ambitious as I am. I think she already sees herself as the executive secretary to the president."

"President?"

"Lawrence Wilson is retiring next year. I'm one of several being considered for the job."

"Oh." Her disappointment sharpened, and she knew she shouldn't feel that way. She should be happy for him. She had the impression being considered for the presidency was something he had worked years to achieve. But she also realized his time would become even more precious. She didn't want to become involved, but she did want some of his time to convince him of the merits of her work project. "No wonder you're so busy."

"Well, thankfully I brought some papers to work on down here. It won't be a total loss."

"Obviously you don't leave home without your briefcase."

A smile crinkled the corners of his eyes as he indicated she leave the living room ahead of him. "I suppose you're right. I don't. Never know when you can snatch a few minutes to work."

In the foyer, she faced him. "You really do have it bad." His attitude confirmed her need to keep her distance emotionally. Her father was a workaholic, and she knew how hard that was on a relationship.

"How so?"

"Here you've been given a golden opportunity to

kick back and relax in a gorgeous setting, and all you can think about is work." The second she saw his smile vanish, his body stiffen, she knew she had overstepped her bounds, but she had always spoken her mind and she wasn't going to stop now even if it meant angering him.

"I grew up here. I've seen it all."

"But I haven't. I've never been to New Orleans. I realize this wasn't part of the date, but can you forget IFI for one day and show me some of the sights after church?" Her heartbeat thundered in her ears; her hands were clammy. She was amazed at her boldness.

"First you talk me into going to a meeting Thursday night and now you want me to show you New Orleans?"

Her gaze coupled with his. "Yes, brazen of me, isn't it?"

"You know, I'm beginning to think your talents are wasted as a teacher. You should have been a negotiator."

"Then you will?"

"Yes."

"In that case, I'll say good-night. It's been a long day." She placed her foot on the first step, intending to escape as quickly as Ruth in case he decided to change his mind.

"Sadie, by the way, did all your wishes come true?"

He was directly behind her, his words a caress. Splinters of awareness shot through her as she slowly turned toward him. They were only inches apart. The silver fire in his eyes unraveled her, sending her heart clamoring. Her teeth sank into her lower lip while she clasped together her damp palms as though they would be an adequate shield between them.

"Did they, Sadie?"

She swallowed several times, afraid her voice wouldn't work when she spoke. "Almost."

"What hasn't come true yet?"

Her throat closed. Her fourth wish swirled in her mind like a kaleidoscope. "Bad luck to say."

"How can I help you if you don't tell me what it is?"

Her gaze slid away from the bright look in his eyes. She focused on a point beyond his shoulder and frantically searched for a way not to tell him what her fourth wish had been.

His finger whispered across her cheek, startling her. Her gaze flew to his face. "I know I shouldn't pry, but you have my curiosity aroused, Sadie. And since I got the impression I was involved in the wishes—"

"I wanted to eat a Cajun meal. I wanted you to support our Special Olympics program and come to the high school on Thursday night."

Sparks of amusement lit his eyes as he looked at her face. "That's not all, Sadie."

She could feel the heat of her blush. Why did her face have to be read like an open book? "You know, you must be a tough negotiator yourself."

"I wouldn't be where I am today if I wasn't." He cut the space between them even more.

Sadie swallowed hard and backed up the stairs. "Well, tomorrow is going to be a busy day so I'd better get to bed." She whirled and fled upstairs, aware of Andrew's gaze on her the whole way.

Swirls of fog obscured Sadie's view from the balcony. Wispy gray fingers slithered among the plants in the garden below, giving the landscape a ghostly appearance. She shivered and hugged herself even though the air was warm and peppered with the scent of flowers. She imagined the history this place could tell if it could speak.

The moment she thought about history her mind turned to her father. She didn't want him to intrude on her time in New Orleans, but for some reason she felt vulnerable, fragile, like a magnolia blossom. It had taken years to toughen herself to her father's expectations of her.

A memory, clear as if it had happened yesterday, imposed itself on her and whisked away what composure she had left. She'd been ten and learning to dive off a springboard. Over and over her father had worked with her to accomplish that feat one afternoon. After one particular attempt when she'd hit the water at an awkward angle and hurt her arm, she'd sat on the side of the pool with tears streaming down her cheeks. She'd rubbed her arm and looked at her father for some support and love. All she could remember was the anger on his face, his feet braced apart, his hands on his hips. He'd ordered her onto the diving board again. He refused to let her quit until she'd attained her goal. No child of his would ever quit, he'd declared, and they had stayed until the sun had gone down and she'd finally dived into the water with perfect form.

A sound penetrated Sadie's mind, whisking her away from her memories. She blinked, focusing on her surroundings, trying to slow the rapid beating of her heart.

"Sadie?"

She turned from the railing and saw Andrew walking toward her. Bold, tall, an imposing figure. She squeezed her eyes shut and wished he would go away—at least until she had control of her emotions. He was invading her life, making it impossible to keep her distance.

"I thought you were in bed." Sadie automatically fell back a few steps when she discovered Andrew dangerously close. Her heartbeat hadn't slowed its frantic pace, and she had to force herself to take deep, calming breaths of the moisture-laden air that smelled of night and flowers.

"And I thought you were asleep."

"I guess neither of us could sleep. Strange beds do that to me." And the fact she couldn't get him out of her mind, she thought, glad her face was in the shadows.

"I was working and came out here to take a break."

"You allow yourself breaks?"

His chuckle was as warm and caressing as the night with its scents of roses and jasmine. "From time to time, especially when I was finding all I was doing was staring at the computer.'' He leaned close and whispered, ''You want to know something? I was even wishing I had put some video games on my laptop.''

''No? Really! Your secret is safe with me. I won't tell a soul that *the* Andrew Knight thought about playing a video game, especially when he should have been working.''

His laughter filled the air. ''You have corrupted me!''

''It must be the late hour. In the clear light of day I'm sure the old Andrew will be back.''

''He better be. I have an important report due in two days.''

Suddenly the lightheartedness evaporated between them replaced by a subtle tension that tautened Andrew's body. Sadie felt it move up him, and she didn't want the businessman to return just yet. ''You said you were from this area?''

''Yes. I grew up near here and went to Tulane for college.''

''May I see where tomorrow?''

''It's not on any tour of New Orleans I know of,'' he said, a strange huskiness in his voice.

Even though she couldn't see his expression clearly in the dim light from her bedroom, she instantly felt the subject of his childhood home was taboo. ''What is on the tour?''

He shrugged. ''What do you want to see?''

"I don't know. I've never been here. You're the tour guide."

"In that case I'll take you to the usual haunts. The French Quarter. The river."

"What did you do for fun when you lived here?"

The tension was no longer subtle. Sadie didn't need to see his face to feel tension seeping from every pore. The night sounds magnified the silence between them.

"I would escape to the bayou."

Escape? Sadie frowned. Visions of all the movies she'd seen located in the bayous flashed across her mind, and she shivered. "That's one place we can skip. Snakes are my least favorite animal. I know they are important in nature's scheme, but I prefer them behind two-inch-thick glass at a zoo." She forced a lightness into her tone, determined to ease the strain that had sprung up between them.

"How do you feel about alligators?"

"I have a healthy respect for their sharp teeth, their slashing tails. You used to see alligators?"

"Yep. We'd go looking for them."

"Why?" Her voice squeaked.

"For the thrill of it."

"When in the world did you pick up the hobbies of golf and reading?"

"When I grew up and became wiser," he said with a laugh.

"I'm not sure if I have."

"I think you've grown up. So it must be the wiser part," he murmured in the dark night.

She tried to think of something to say. But for once

she was speechless. Definitely the wise part. If she were wise, she would have never come to New Orleans. If she were wise, she wouldn't be out here on the balcony with a man who had stolen into her life in a few short days. If she were wise, she would be on the next flight out of here regardless of its destination.

The blackness seemed to close around Andrew and her, heightening her perception of him. She tried to inhale deep breaths, but each one was infused with his scent of sandalwood. The intensity of the moment was almost tangible, as if Sadie could grab it and hold it in her palm.

He moved toward her, his arm brushing hers. ''Do you ever do things just for the thrill of it?'' he asked, his question loaded with a hazardous potency she knew she should avoid.

She stepped back, coming up against a column. ''Yes.''

''Do you like to take risks?''

''Yes—within reason.''

''Within reason? What limits do you set for yourself?''

He was a breath away, and she couldn't think with any kind of reason at all. She frantically searched her mind for an answer, but all she could think about was his nearness. Somehow she knew he was in a dangerous mood, as if he were challenging her to try to invade his privacy.

''When I take a risk, there has to be a reasonable chance it's worth it.'' She licked her lips nervously.

"And if you find out it's not after plunging in, what do you do?" He bent closer, one arm braced on the column near her head.

"I cut my losses. I'm a risk taker, not a fool." She hoped, she added silently, wondering if being here was a step in that direction.

"Interesting. I don't take risks in my life except in business."

"Why not? I don't see you afraid of much." Again she wet her lips, her teeth nibbling on the lower one.

"We all have our fears, Sadie. But to answer your question, I take so many in my professional life that there's nothing left for my personal one."

"Show me where you grew up." She threw the challenge out to defuse the charged moment, to force him to back off.

"You do like to take risks, don't you?"

Sadie gulped, sparks of danger charging the air. "Risks are what make me feel alive. Living would be boring if I never did anything a little daring. Once when I was careening down a mountain slope I wasn't ready to handle, my life flashed before my eyes. It didn't take long. I made it to the bottom and vowed there would be more than school in my life. I became active in my church. Took up several sports other than skiing. I decided to go to college and do what *I* wanted, not what my father wished for me."

"I had expected a yes or no answer." He chuckled, smoothing a strand of her hair behind her ear. "You're a woman of many words."

"Especially when I'm nervous." The high pitch of

her voice conveyed her nervousness while she felt paralyzed against the column.

"I make you nervous?"

"Don't sound so surprised. I think you're aware of your effect on me."

His chuckle danced on the warm air again. "I do like your honesty, Sadie Spencer."

A blush tinted her cheeks. She hadn't lied to him, but she hadn't told him the whole truth concerning why she had sought him out for a date. She would have to find the right moment and tell him soon before she lost her heart to him.

Andrew pulled away completely and grabbed her hand. "Let's go for a ride."

"Where?"

"You wanted to see where I grew up. I'll show you."

She stood her ground, forcing him to turn toward her. "Are you sure you want to?"

He shook his head. "You just asked me twice to show you and now you don't want to go. Make up your mind."

She straightened. "I sensed it wasn't something you wanted to do. I was just trying to be sensitive to you."

"I didn't want to at first. Now I do. A guy can change his mind."

"Why?"

"I'm not sure why, Sadie. I don't usually look backward. Maybe being here is the reason. Maybe it's you. I haven't shared my childhood with many."

"Then I'd be honored to see the house you grew up in."

"Actually we have two places to visit." His hold tightened around her hand.

"Just two. You were lucky. My father taught at several colleges before coming to Cimarron City University. We moved around a lot while I was growing up."

"Then we have something else in common. I did, too," he said, a strain in his voice that transmitted pain. "But these two places are the only ones that count."

Sadie stood staring at the vacant lot, overgrown, with the remains of a chimney poking through the lush undergrowth, and her heart throbbed with a slow beat. A lump was wedged in her throat, making any comment difficult.

"I haven't been able to sell this place. I should," Andrew said in a monotone as if he were reliving every horrendous moment. "I was ten when it happened. We were all asleep when the fire broke out. I got out. My parents and younger sister didn't. I watched as the flames destroyed my life."

Knowing words couldn't comfort, Sadie took his hand in hers and squeezed gently, letting the silence lengthen between them, the sound of crickets chirping filling the void.

"After that I was shuffled among half a dozen foster families over the next several years. I wasn't an easy boy to deal with. I had a lot of anger inside of me.''

''You had no family?''

''No one who would take in a rebellious ten-year-old.'' He stared at the chimney, deep in thought. ''Actually when I reached high school, I was put with Tom Dawson, and my whole life was changed.'' A smile graced his mouth for a few seconds before vanishing. ''It wasn't easy at first. But Tom wouldn't give up on me. He made me understand that God had his reasons for sparing my life in the fire and that it was useless to fight His plan. I started going to the church where he was a pastor. For two years I had a relatively normal life, until…'' His voice trailed off into nothingness.

''What happened?''

''For the second time in my life God took my family away. After that I gave up on having a family.''

''And God?''

''I found it was better to rely only on myself. It's worked for the past twenty years just fine.''

''Has it?'' While she had been struggling to make her father accept her, failures and all, Andrew had had a far different childhood. Anguish twisted in her chest.

He turned toward her, grasping her other hand in his. ''I didn't tell you this for your pity. My childhood toughened me. I don't let my emotions govern me and I'm much better off.''

''Are you?''

''Yes.''

"Why are you telling me this then? Are you warning me?"

"Yes." He inched closer. "I'm thirty-seven years old and have never been seriously involved with anyone. My work is my life and that is the way I've wanted it."

She didn't back away even though with each sentence he came a little nearer. She had spent a good part of her life trying to please her father and always failing. She had watched her mother doing the same thing. She had vowed years ago never to go through that again. Coming in second in a relationship was unacceptable to her. "Then you have nothing to worry about. My emotions are all tied up with my class. I have fifteen students who need me. I have no need for any other kind of relationship in my life except friendship."

"You know why I'm running away. Why are you, Sadie?"

Chapter Four

How could she tell Andrew she was afraid to commit because of her parents, especially her father? Sadie wondered, remembering Andrew's story about his parents and the anguish he experienced losing them. With her fingers linked through his, she stared at the crumbling chimney and tried to form the words to explain her fear.

He released her hands and shifted away from her. "I'm sorry. I shouldn't have asked. I just warned you about me and then I turn around and ask such a personal question. Our—acquaintance doesn't warrant that."

Acquaintance, not relationship or even friendship. Closing her eyes for a few seconds, she could almost imagine the smell of the fire that had torn his life in two. He deserved an answer. She sucked in a deep breath of moisture-laden air and said, "I grew up in a home with both parents, but it was difficult being raised by a father who demanded perfection from me and my mother. I could never do anything to please him. I tried. I really did." Tears stung her eyes. She choked back the lump of emotions rising in her throat. She'd never told anyone else that, and surprisingly it felt right.

The stillness magnified the importance of what had happened. His expression showed disquieting astonishment, as if he couldn't quite believe they both had ignored years of holding secrets to reveal something of themselves.

Andrew drew her against him. "I propose no more journeys into the past. I know you didn't come on this date to relive bad memories. I certainly didn't. We look forward from here on out."

Listening to the steady beat of his heart soothed her tattered nerves. "Sounds like a deal to me. Where do we go from here?"

"I was going to show you Tom's house, but that's the past. Are you sleepy?"

She shook her head, leaning to look into his face. The gray light of dawn fingered across the eastern sky, declaring a new day.

"Neither am I." A smile graced his mouth. "I know a café not far from here that serves wonderful beignets and coffee New Orleans style. They used to make the best beignets in these parts. Do you think you're up for that?"

"Are you kidding? You can't come to New Orleans and not sample one, and some chicory coffee, too."

It was a fifteen-minute drive to the small café. Its gray exterior with broken pieces of wood in the railing of the porch proclaimed it had seen better days. But inside, the place was spotless, the chrome shined and the wood polished. Sadie noticed the café was already crowded, and the sun had just risen. Sliding into a booth across from Andrew, she looked out the picture window at the golden light spreading rapidly across the landscape. Through the branches of the large live oak tree with Spanish moss draped on its limbs, the sun illuminated the sky in streaks of orange, rose and yellow.

She stifled a yawn. "I know I'm going to regret this. I haven't stayed up all night like this in years—since college when I had to study for my finals."

"A cup of chicory coffee ought to keep you up." Andrew gave their order to the waitress who stopped by the table on the way to the booth next to them. "I think I can remember pulling a few all-nighters back in my college days, even though that seems a lifetime ago."

"You're not *that* old." Sadie smiled at the harried waitress as she poured their cups full of the steaming coffee, then rushed away.

"I sometimes feel older than my thirty-seven years."

"Then you should teach high schoolers. They keep me young."

"Now *I* have to say *you* aren't that old."

"I figure I'll be saying that when I grow old and gray-headed." Taking a sip of her brew, Sadie relished the strong flavor that indeed would help keep her awake.

The waitress slapped the plates of beignets on the table and hurried to another booth. The bell over the door chimed as more customers came into the café. The smell of coffee and fried food infused the air while the sounds of different conversations floated to Sadie.

She allowed her beignet to cool for a minute, then gingerly picked it up between her thumb and forefinger. She took a breath, and white confectioners' sugar flew everywhere.

"Oh, my, you should have warned me," she said with a laugh, noticing the powder adorning the black shirt she'd borrowed from Ruth.

"And miss the initiation?" Andrew raised a brow as he carefully took a bite of his beignet.

After tucking a napkin into her shirt like a bib, Sadie savored the sweet taste of her food between sips of coffee. The tastes complemented each other, making this New Orleans breakfast an experience she would remember. But she knew the main reason she would remember and relish this trip was the man sitting across from her.

When she'd finished three beignets, he asked, "Want any more?"

She shook her head.

He reached across the table and brushed the side of her cheek with his napkin. "You still had some sugar there. I think in the short time I've known you I've had more breakfasts than in all of last year."

Sadie glanced at her empty plate with a dusting of white all over it. "I don't think we should classify this as a true breakfast, or the one I fixed you last weekend. One day I'll prepare you what I consider a true breakfast." The second she extended the invitation she wished she could retract it. She bit the inside of her cheek to keep from making the situation any worse.

His gaze captured hers. "I just might have to take you up on that when my life settles down."

"After the fight for the presidency?"

"Yes."

"You think your life will be simpler then?"

"I hope so."

"That doesn't sound like a man eager to take on more."

"I'm a man eager to move on to the next challenge."

"And work is the only challenge you see?"

His jaw clenched, a nerve in his cheek twitching. "Yes—and that's the way I like it."

He might as well be wearing an off-limits sign around his neck. Sadie finished the last sip of coffee. "I find my work a challenge, but I like to balance it with other things. I enjoy my church and coaching Special Olympics." She lifted her arm to glance at her watch. "Speaking of church, when does it start? I don't want to hold up Ruth and Darrell."

Andrew tossed some money on the table. "I'm not sure, so we'd better go. I don't want to hold them up, either. I've faced Ruth's wrath before, and it's an experience I would like to forgo.''

The quaint small church, freshly painted white with forest green trim, sat nestled among live oaks, tall pines and magnolia trees. As soon as Darrell pulled into the parking lot at the side of the building, Sadie felt waves of tension emanating from Andrew, who was next to her in the back seat.

Carrie leaped from the car while Darrell and Ruth gathered up their belongings and followed their daughter. Andrew remained in the back seat, the taut set of his shoulders and his fisted hands indicating something was terribly wrong.

Sadie slipped her hand over his clenched one. ''Want to tell me about it?''

''Tom was the pastor of this church. I attended it when I was young.''

''And you haven't been back?''

''Could never bring myself to. I don't think I can go inside.''

''Do you want me to sit with you?''

''No.'' His answer was clipped, said through clamped teeth. He sucked in a deep breath, held it for a moment then released it slowly. ''No, it's about time I put the past behind me.''

Sadie laced her fingers through his and walked beside him up the stairs and into the church. Everyone was standing and singing the opening hymn, the rafters of the sanctuary vibrating with the sweet tones of

"Amazing Grace." Immediately Sadie felt at ease, as though she'd come home.

The inside was simply decorated. The most ornate aspect was the eight stained-glass windows depicting scenes from the Old Testament. Light poured in through the floor-to-ceiling windows and danced on the polished wooden floor. Lemon wax and various perfumes scented the air. Sadie scanned the church for the Madisons.

Andrew's grip on her hand tightened as the organ swelled for the final notes of the song. Sadie slanted a look toward him and noticed the tense set to his expression, the taut line of his body and wondered if he would stay. Indecision played across his features.

The hymn ended, and the congregation began to sit. Sadie spied Darrell and motioned to Andrew. He again fortified himself with a bracing breath and moved down the center aisle toward the middle. Her heart ached with what Andrew must be going through. Wrestling with memories was hard, and she suspected he didn't often do it. To him the past wasn't something to relive.

The service flew by. Sadie enjoyed the sermon about overcoming fear. The pastor quoted Isaiah 41:13. "For I the Lord thy God will hold thy right hand, saying unto thee, Fear not; I will help thee." She felt Andrew's fingers close about hers. The gentle pressure of his touch through the rest of the sermon brought tears to her eyes. By the time she sang the final hymn, she had herself under control.

At the end Andrew hung back and let everyone else

file out, even Darrell and his family. He told them he would be along in a moment. His friend took one look at Andrew's expression and nodded.

Sadie stood beside Andrew, searching for the right words to say. *Lord, how do I help him through this?*

When the church was empty, Andrew sank down onto the pew, his shoulders hunched, his head drooping. Sadie reached out to lay her hand on him, but didn't. She didn't have the right to intrude, and yet she realized she wished she did. Instead, she dropped her arm to her side and bowed her head. *Heavenly Father, give me the insight I need. He is hurting, and I want to be there for him.*

The silence of the church echoed through Sadie's mind. In the distance she heard the murmurs of the congregation just outside the open double doors. The cool autumn breeze blew in, carrying with it the hint of moisture and honeysuckle. She waited, still not sure what she could do to ease Andrew's burden.

He lifted his head and stared at the altar. "I should have come back before this."

"Why didn't you?"

"I didn't know if I could handle it. Now I know I can." His gaze swung to hers. "I can put my past behind me, where it belongs, once and for all. I've let it control me more than I thought. Now it won't."

The tone and finality of his words took her by surprise.

"I should be angry at Darrell and Ruth. They didn't tell me they went to this church."

"Perhaps they didn't realize how much it affected you."

"We went to high school together. They knew."

"Then they thought it was time you dealt with what happened to Tom."

"Death is what happened to Tom. It's that simple."

"Is it?"

"I learned early not to care too much." Anger, suppressed but under the surface, sounded in his voice as he fought to erase any emotion in his expression.

"Then why did it bother you to come back here?" she asked, realizing she was intruding on his private life.

"Memories." His grin was lopsided, self-mocking. "I guess I'm mortal, like everyone else. Until Darrell pulled up to this church, I didn't realize just how much it would affect me. Now that I think about it, I probably wouldn't have said anything to him at the house. I would have shrugged and thought it wasn't a big deal."

"But it was?"

His look was sharp. It pierced her. "Yes, it was, but not now. Tom is gone. My family is gone. There's nothing I can do about those facts. But I can't let them govern my life."

"So they won't? I wish I could get a handle on my life that easily."

"Life moves forward, not backward."

The determination in his voice underscored his feelings more than the words he'd spoken. Sadie wished she could separate her past from the present, from the future. But who she was was wrapped up in that past. And the same was true for Andrew. What was going to happen when his past finally caught up with him and he was forced to deal with it?

"I have goals, plans."

"What about God in all those plans? Have you made peace with Him today?"

"I'm not at war with Him." Andrew surged to his feet.

"Then you don't blame Him for your family and Tom's deaths?" She rose, standing only a foot from him.

"I don't blame Him. I don't depend on Him, either. God exists. That's all."

"It's that simple," Sadie countered, wanting to shake some sense into the man.

"Simple? Life isn't simple. Death is, but not life." Andrew signaled with a wave of his hand for Sadie to step to the center aisle. "Darrell and Ruth will wonder what's happened to us. We'd better leave."

Sadie saw his closed expression and knew he'd shut down his emotions. He was very good at doing that. Coming to New Orleans opened a door on his past that he usually was very successful at keeping locked.

The breeze from the river ruffled the stray strands of Sadie's hair, making them dance, enticing her to let down her guard and relish the beautiful day. She loved being on the water. The sounds of a steamboat cutting a path toward a far-off pier and a gull over-head insinuated their way into her mind. She relaxed against the railing…

"It's not that difficult, Sadie, to learn to ski. I don't have all day." Her father's words rang above the roar of the motorboat. *"This is the last time. If you can't get up, that's it."*

Her limbs ached with fatigue. She squinted and tried to make out the figure of her father, leaning over the side of the boat as he shoved the loose ski toward her. The glare of the sun caused her eyes to burn. She saw the ski slide past her and grabbed for it. She missed, her hand grabbing a fist full of water.

"Sadie, hurry up. It's getting late."

She swam toward the ski and struggled into it. Her arms shook. Her legs felt as though they were made of rubber. But she would stand up on the skis this time or—

She wouldn't complete the thought. She would just do it. Her father didn't allow for any option but success. And he didn't like to waste time obtaining that success.

The boat darted forward. Her arms jerked straight. She locked her elbows and prayed.

When she rose out of the water, she wanted to shout her joy. She wobbled. Tensing, she focused all her attention on staying up for longer than a second.

Minutes later she crashed into the water. Elated that she'd finally gotten up on her skis after only four tries, she was ready to go again. She wanted to fly over the wake like her friend Sally did.

"We need to head back, Sadie. Come on in." Her father reached out to help her into the boat.

She whipped the wet hair out of her eyes and grasped her father's hand. "I did it!"

Her father didn't say a word. All Sadie could remember was the frown carved deep into his tanned features as he hoisted her out of the water....

The sound of the steamboat's horn jolted Sadie from her memories. Leaning on the white railing, she watched the people on the pier and tried to compose herself before having to face Andrew.

He shifted next to her. "You were a million miles away," he murmured close to her ear.

"No, just a journey into the past." She glanced at him and saw the puzzled expression in his eyes. "I guess this is a day for that."

"I thought this was your first trip to New Orleans?"

"It is. But it's not my first time being on a river." She hoped her crisp tone conveyed her reluctance to discuss her past. They each had memories they didn't want to delve too far into.

"What did you think of this ride?"

"I could get used to this mode of transportation. It's slow, relaxing. I like listening to the paddle wheel. Sorta like a waterfall. I could fall asleep listening to it." She twisted to face him squarely. "I doubt I'll be very good tomorrow at school. Think we can bottle this sound and play it later on our way home?"

He smiled. "I'll check the musical repertoire on

the plane. Maybe there's something that'll help. But to tell you the truth I don't even know if it has a sound system.''

''You don't?''

''I'm always working.''

''The story of your life?''

Momentarily a dark storm edged into his expression. ''There's nothing wrong with that.''

''I think we've had this discussion about all work and no play. I have no intentions of trying to change you.''

''You don't?'' Skepticism was evident in his question and the lift of his brow.

''Nope. You're a big boy now. If you want to work your life away, that's your business. Of course, at the end of a day you might ask yourself what you'll have for it in, say, twenty years.''

Andrew didn't reply but turned away as if he were interested in watching the docking process. Sadie thought he was going to ignore what she'd said until he looked at her and declared, ''After I get the presidency, I'll have that time to play.''

She arched a brow, much as he had a moment before. ''You will? You keep saying that. Are you sure you won't just substitute another goal that will drive you to work even harder?''

His frown furrowed his brow, his lips compressed into a slash. ''I think it's time for us to leave the boat.''

He started to walk toward the gangplank. Sadie placed a hand on his arm to halt him. ''Forget what

I've said, Andrew. I don't want those careless re-marks to dampen the rest of the afternoon. I've had such a good time so far. The French Quarter was won-derful. Everything I thought it would be. Is it a deal? Next time you can just put your hand over my mouth to stop me from putting my foot in it.''

The tension eased from his shoulders. He stuck his hand out for her to shake. ''That's a deal I'll accept. Now let me understand. I can put my hand over your mouth anytime I think you're going to stick your foot into it?''

She narrowed her eyes in mock anger. ''No. Only when referring to your diligent work habits and non-existent play—''

He pressed his hand over her mouth, the rough tex-ture of his palm warm against the softness of her lips. ''You were saying?''

She glared at him and mumbled, ''Funny.''

''I try to be, in rare moments of playfulness.'' He hooked his arm through hers and began to lead her toward the gangplank.

''Then you think I should savor this rare mo-ment?''

''Funny,'' he said, mimicking her tone and look. ''We need to hurry if we're going to make this next stop before it's too late.''

She glanced at her watch. ''It's a little early for dinner. Where are we going?''

''Why do you think I'm going to tell you when I haven't all afternoon? I like to surprise you.''

''Did I tell you I hated surprises? I actually open

all my Christmas presents ahead of time then rewrap them so no one knows.''

His laughter filled the air with a richness she could get used to. "I think my family figured it out, though. They don't bother to wrap them anymore. They just give me mine in a bag with a token amount of tissue to cover the gift.''

"I can just picture you getting up when everyone else in the family is asleep and sneaking into the living room to open your gifts.''

"That's why my parents could never get me to sleep on Christmas Eve. I couldn't wait for Santa Claus and those presents I didn't know about. It used to kill me. My curiosity is a horrible burden I must bear.''

"Somehow that doesn't surprise me.''

"Do I note a touch of sarcasm?''

"Never from my lips.''

Darrell and Ruth's driver was waiting for them by the curb. Sadie had a strong suspicion the man knew Andrew's plans. The driver went about his duties in silence as though Andrew had mapped out everything before they had started. Of course, he had. Andrew wouldn't know any other way to do it. Spontaneity wasn't in his vocabulary. She would have to see if she could change that—at least for this one day.

When they pulled up to a tall building by the Mississippi, Sadie wasn't sure what to expect. When they arrived at the Top of the Mart, Sadie was charmed by the spectacular view it offered of New Orleans. She saw the wide river winding through the Crescent City, the haze that clung to the horizon. The late afternoon sun was sinking in the west as they were shown to a table. The day's shadows lengthened over the city as though they were fingers reaching out to all its parts.

"This is beautiful. What a way to see a place." Sadie craned to look as far as she could.

"This is definitely a different perspective of New Orleans than the one a person gets from the French Quarter or the river."

"It's romantic. I didn't know you had it in you," she said without thinking, regretting the words the second they were out of her mouth.

"Ouch, I think."

"What I mean is that you are so practical and..." Her voice faded into silence as her gaze found his.

She looked away, forcing herself to concentrate on the sights of New Orleans at dusk. The yellow-orange western horizon set the sky on fire. Streaks of various shades of red ribboned across the heavens like streamers on a colorful package, enticing her to open it.

The silence between them lasted until after the waitress took their orders. When Andrew leaned forward, his words returned her attention to his face. "I have to admit that I don't usually have time to be, as you say, romantic. But in New Orleans I find it easier. This city lends itself to romance."

"Yes, it does have a certain flair."

"But you are right about me being practical. I'm a businessman first and foremost."

She heard the warning in his voice. "Are you saying a businessman can't be romantic? Is there something you take in college that wipes that from your system?"

"No, I believe it's in my genes. You're right, I can't speak for other businessmen."

His chuckle flowed over her, and she wished again that he would laugh more. Sadie liked the way he relaxed when he smiled. His whole face lit, warming every inch of her. "Being practical doesn't mean you can't be romantic. I would say being romantic was very practical. A few romantic gestures can go a long way in a relationship. That can make life much easier, don't you think?"

"I'll keep that in mind when I have time for a relationship."

"Ah, yes. Your fight for the presidency. Why do you want to be the president of the company?"

His eyes widened. He waited until after the waitress had placed their coffee in front of them before answering. "Why not? I've done just about everything else I wanted to at IFI. It's the next logical step."

"You sound like a restless man. Never satisfied with what you have."

"You make ambition sound like a dirty word."

"Are you satisfied?"

"Yes," he answered without a thought. "If I weren't, I wouldn't be doing what I'm doing. There's one thing I don't do. I don't waste my time."

"Has today been a waste?" Sadie couldn't believe she was asking the question, but often, to her regret, she spoke her mind.

His probing look snared hers. He brought his cup

to his mouth and took a sip, never breaking eye contact with her. "No. Contrary to what you believe, I sometimes do recognize the need to get away from the office."

Sadie was the one to look away first. She studied the darkening landscape of New Orleans, which glittered with lights. It reminded her of Christmas, her favorite holiday.

"In fact, Sadie, I'm grateful that you stayed. I'd forgotten what New Orleans could be like. I've enjoyed seeing my birthplace through your eyes."

The warmth in his regard robbed her of coherent thought. From across a crowded room, his gaze had a way of drawing her toward him, and suddenly she was frightened by the power this man was beginning to have over her. She had never given another human being that kind of power since she had given up trying to prove herself to her father. She prided herself on being her own person, never depending on anyone for emotional support. But the newfound feelings swirling inside of her were making a mockery of that declaration. Were she and Andrew more alike than she cared to acknowledge? Neither wanted to admit depending on another. But whereas he prided himself on standing totally alone, she sought the Lord's guidance.

When they left the restaurant in the French Quarter, Sadie took a deep breath of the cool night air, enhanced with Cajun spices and the scent of the river nearby. "I'm stuffed. That was delicious."

Andrew started to guide her toward the limousine waiting by the curb, but she hung back. "I need to walk this dinner off, Andrew. We're not far from the river. When do we have to be at the airport?"

"The plane doesn't have to be back until tomorrow morning."

"You mean we could stay out all night," she whispered as though she were a teenager plotting to foil her parents.

"I thought you had school tomorrow."

"I do, and I suppose after not sleeping much last night I would regret it. But it's fun to defy the laws of nature every once in a while."

Andrew walked to the driver, said a few words to the man, then came back to Sadie. "I told him to take my luggage to the plane and to tell the pilot we'll be a while longer. We'll take a cab when the mood strikes us to leave. What do you want to do? It's your turn to show me what you want."

It took a supreme effort for Sadie to keep her mouth from dropping open. "What about your plans?"

He snapped his fingers. "Erased."

"At the stroke of midnight you aren't going to turn into a pumpkin?"

"No. And I suspect I require less sleep than you do."

She tucked her arm through his, liking the feel of him at her side. "Then let's walk. I believe I remember that Jackson Square isn't too far from here."

When they arrived at Jackson Square, Sadie surveyed the crowd of people milling about, the artists displaying their work, some musicians entertaining the tourists with the blues. The aroma of various foods vying for dominance saturated the air. The sounds of laughter and conversations wafted to her. "I want something to take back to Cimarron City. Let's get our portrait drawn."

"Together?"

"Yes, cheaper that way." Sadie tugged on his arm.

After negotiating a price for their portrait, Andrew sat slightly behind her and to the right. "I hope this doesn't take too long. I'm not very good at just sitting," he whispered into her ear, sending tingles down her neck.

"Why doesn't that surprise me? Now be good. This isn't a painful process."

Ten minutes later Sadie had her doubts about that. It was pure torture to be sitting so close to Andrew, breathing in his clean scent, which mingled with the aromas of the river, Cajun spices and flowers in the park. Feeling him along her back and side, she decided this was definitely not a good idea and scooted away from him. His hand clamped on her shoulder and stopped her movement.

"Sit still. I thought I was the one with the problem," he whispered. "I don't want to have to sit here any longer than necessary."

Andrew started to remove his hand from her when the young man drawing the portrait said, "No. I like that better. Drape your arm like this." He came up to them and positioned Andrew's arm along hers so he cradled her to him, as though they had been friends a long time.

Okay, so she had made it worse rather than better by trying to put some space between them. She could do this. Surely it wouldn't last much longer—she hoped. But ten minutes later her nerves were as taut as a stretched rubber band about to snap. She was tired. That had to be the reason for this unusual reaction to Andrew, that and the spell New Orleans had cast on her.

"There. Done," the man said, a smile of satisfaction on his young face.

Sadie was almost afraid to look at the portrait. She knew what she would see, and she was disconcerted when she finally stood and peered at the drawing. The dreamy expression on her face spoke volumes that she wished she could have masked, but she had always been easy to read. A burden she had to bear, she decided as she slanted a glance at Andrew to gauge his reaction.

He studied the portrait, his brow knitted with a thoughtful expression as if he had just discovered something he wasn't sure about. She knew that feeling. The portrait before them showed a couple who looked perfect together, a couple who belonged together, two halves of a whole. What had been captured on the canvas in such a short time exposed her to the world, and that bothered her more than she cared to acknowledge. This definitely hadn't been one of her better ideas. All she wanted Andrew to do was pay the young man, wrap the portrait up and never peer at it again.

"Do we have time for one more thing?" Sadie asked when they were walking away from the man who had drawn their picture.

"I'm afraid to say yes for fear of what you'll come up with. After all, you were the one who bid on me at the auction just so you could see me about Special Olympics. That should have given me a hint when you told me that. And to think I turned the rest of the evening over to you."

She waited until it was clear to cross the street before answering him. "I just want to see the river at night. There's nothing wrong with that."

Again she was proven wrong when, a few minutes later, she was standing on the Moonwalk by the edge of the river enfolded in a velvety night, the cool breeze stirring the strands of her hair, the scents of beignets and coffee drifting to her from a café not far away. She shivered.

"Cold?"

She didn't reply. Andrew drew her against his length and enveloped her in his arms. She felt as though she had come home in his embrace. Oh, no, she was in trouble again.

"We probably better leave," she murmured, the statement not coming out with any force while her gaze was transfixed by the romantic spill of moonlight on the river.

"Yeah, probably." His whispered words were close to her ear, tickling its shell.

Neither made a move to leave.

She snuggled against him, seeking his warmth. He hugged her closer. The stars, the river, the night cast their magic over her, making her believe anything was possible. And maybe for this one day, it was. Tomorrow they would be in Cimarron City, and life would proceed.

When he turned her to face him, she didn't say a word. Instead, she tilted her head to look into his eyes, hidden in the shadows of night that had woven a spell around them. This was not reality, Sadie repeated silently. They wanted different things from life. They led different lives. And yet, she was drawn to him. She wanted to heal his broken heart, help him see that God hadn't abandoned him all those years ago.

Andrew cupped her face, his fingers combing through her hair. "I enjoyed myself, Sadie."

"But?"

"But we need to leave for the airport. Tomorrow we'll regret staying so long in New Orleans."

Regret? No, she doubted she ever would. "When we're at work trying to stay awake?"

"Yes, exactly." He stepped away, his arms falling to his sides.

Somehow she didn't think that was what he'd really meant. He was already reining in his emotions, closing totally down. She didn't have to see his expression to know how he looked. She could tell by his distancing, his stance that held him apart.

Chapter Five

The second the seat belt snapped closed, the strap secure about Sadie's hips, she felt trapped, perspiration beading on her upper lip. She gripped the arms of her chair and stared straight ahead. The plane began to taxi to the end of the runway. Her fingernails dug into the cushioned padding.

Breathe, she told herself, but the tightness in her chest attested to the fact she couldn't. *Remember the pastor's sermon today about fear.*

"Sadie, are you okay?"

Andrew's question seemed to come from afar, as though he spoke to her from the other end of a long tunnel. Her mind was blank. She was unable to form a coherent sentence. *The fear of man bringeth a snare: but whoso putteth his trust in the Lord shall be safe.* The words from Proverbs 29:25 gave her the strength to turn toward Andrew and offer him a ghost of a smile.

He covered her hand with his, rubbing his warm palm across the backs of her fingers. "Are you afraid of flying?"

"I'm trying not to be."

"I thought you were a risk taker."

"Only when I am in control. I thought about learning to fly—but only for a millisecond."

"That long?"

"Okay, we've established I'm afraid of flying. Please let's not talk about it anymore." Again she recited silently the words from the Bible and again she felt more capable of dealing with this fear.

"Whatever you say." Andrew continued to massage her hand as though he could impart his courage into her. "What would you like to talk about? The weather?"

"Not at the moment, since it directly affects flying," she quipped, glad she could joke about her fear.

"Then tell me about Thursday night. What do you expect me to do?"

She focused her thoughts on her plan to get Andrew involved with her students. For a moment it took her mind away from the fact that the plane was barreling down the runway. "This is an organizational meeting. I want you—" The jet lifted off the ground, and Sadie choked back her next words.

"Don't leave me hanging in suspense, Sadie. You can't say that to a man and not complete the sentence." He pried her hand loose from the padded arm and held it cradled between his palms.

The plane's ascent left her breathless, her heart

speeding as fast as the jet through the air. Sweat popped out on her forehead and rolled down her face. *I am not alone. God is with me.*

"Take a deep breath, Sadie. You look like you're going to faint. How in the world did you make it to New Orleans?"

Sadie followed his advice, and slowly her lungs filled with stale air and her heart eased its frantic beating. "I prayed a lot. I hate to fall apart around others."

"But with me it's okay?"

"Something like that. You should be flattered. I feel comfortable enough around you to fall apart."

"Thanks, I think."

She felt his gaze on her and turned to meet his look. "You're welcome."

The jet leveled off, and her body's reaction to the fact they were thousands of feet in the air settled into a slight case of the nerves. She wiped her free hand across her forehead and upper lip.

She attempted a smile that quivered about the corners of her mouth for a few seconds before disappearing. "I'm not afraid of many things, but flying is one of them. I'm okay, usually, between takeoffs and landings."

"So we have a few hours."

"If the weather holds."

"So what do you expect of me on Thursday?"

"I want you to present the check from IFI and say a few words. That's all. You don't have to stay, but

I would love for you to have pizza with us afterward. That is, if you have the time.''

"Pizza? Isn't that fattening? I'm surprised a teacher who teaches nutrition would encourage such a dish.''

Sadie responded to the teasing tone in his voice with a laugh. "Pizza covers four of the five food groups. If you happen to like pineapple on your pizza, it can cover all five. I think that's pretty nutritious. Besides, you work with what you've got. Teenagers have distinct appetites and are particularly attracted to sugar and fats.''

"Then I'll be at the high school at seven with a check, a few words and an appetite for pizza.'' He unlatched his seat belt and shifted in the chair to a more comfortable position. "Now that the date is almost over, what was your fourth wish?''

The question caught her by surprise. Her eyes widened, and her throat went dry. She remembered her foolish fourth wish, to be kissed by him, and blushed. "Nothing to concern you.'' She squeaked the words out.

"I don't believe you, Sadie. You're ten shades of red.''

"Okay. It does concern you. But that's all you're going to find out.'' She pressed her lips closed to emphasize her point.

"Oh, now you have my curiosity aroused. You know I'm not going to let this drop.''

She narrowed her eyes and folded her arms across her chest.

He laughed. "I think I get the hint. Okay, if you

won't tell me what it is, then at least tell me when it is fulfilled.''

She nodded, feeling the heat in her cheeks spreading. She needed to get their conversation away from wishes and onto a safer topic. ''I had two reasons for bidding on you at the auction. One was IFI supporting our Special Olympics team, and the other—'' she heaved a sigh and plunged ahead ''—the other involved a vocational training program I'm developing at the high school.''

Andrew stiffened, his expression neutral.

''I have a student who will be graduating this year.'' She hurried ahead with her explanation before she lost her nerve. ''I would like to place him in a job in the community before he leaves high school. He's a wonderful, hard worker who would be an asset to any company that hired him.''

''And you want IFI to hire him?''

''If I can get the biggest employer in Cimarron City to participate in the program, others will follow. I want to try him out on a trial basis for a few hours each afternoon. There's a funding source that will pay his salary while he's training.''

''What if it doesn't work out?''

''Then you don't hire him after graduation. But if you agreed to this program, it would be with the serious intention of hiring him when he's out of high school.''

''Is this why you couldn't get by Mrs. Fox?''

''Yes.''

He frowned, rubbing the back of his neck. "I don't know about this, Sadie."

"Please meet Chris first before you decide."

"Will he be there Thursday night?"

She nodded.

"Now I know why you didn't take your donation and just buy uniforms."

"What I said was true. We need a sponsor, but I won't kid you. My main reason for betting on you was for Chris. If I didn't think this would benefit everyone, especially IFI, I wouldn't have pursued it so vigorously. I just need a chance to prove this job program can work and my students can be a valuable asset to a company."

"This means a lot to you."

It wasn't a question, but she said yes anyway.

"So this whole date was really work to you?"

"It started out that way, but quickly changed last night."

"When?"

"When you took me to see your home."

Silence descended between them, the hum of the engines the only sound.

"You know, I should be angry with you. But how can I be when you've just proven you're more like me than you think?"

"How so?"

"Your work—your students—they're very important to you. Your life revolves around them, I suspect."

"I do have a balance."

"And I don't?"

"What do you think?"

"I don't." He lifted his briefcase onto his lap and opened it. "Which reminds me, I have work to do."

Sadie watched him shuffle through some papers before he pulled out a stack of them. He had effectively shut a door in her face, and she couldn't blame him. She was afraid her plan had backfired.

"That concludes our business. Now I would like to introduce Mr. Andrew Knight from IFI, who has an announcement for us." Smiling at Andrew, Sadie stepped to the side.

He walked to the podium in the high school auditorium and waited for the applause to die down before saying, "Miss Spencer, I appreciate the opportunity to come here tonight and present Cimarron High School Special Olympics team with a check from IFI for two thousand dollars. We are proud to be a sponsor of such a fine endeavor."

Surprised at the generous amount, Sadie took the check from Andrew while her students and their parents cheered and clapped. "On behalf of the team, I want to thank IFI for their support and you for coming tonight." After shaking his hand, she continued, "I hope to see everyone at Mitchell's for pizza."

Several of her students swarmed her and Andrew, wanting to see the check. Sadie held it up for them to look at it, then said, "I don't know about you all, but I'm starved."

"Me, too," a small girl who didn't weigh more than eighty pounds said.

"Does this mean we get new shirts?"

"Chris, this means we get new uniforms." Sadie folded the check and put it into her pocket.

"New ones?" A tall, thin boy with freckles and a ready smile asked.

"Yes, Kevin."

"In time for soccer?" Chris asked, his optimistic gaze fixed on Andrew.

"Not for soccer, but hopefully in time for basketball. Our soccer tournament is next week." Sadie began walking toward the back of the auditorium, where some of the parents were waiting for their children.

Andrew slowed his pace, allowing the students to go ahead of them. "Is that the Chris you want to work at IFI?"

"Yes. He's twenty." Sadie stopped halfway up the center aisle, realizing Chris's small stature might make him appear younger to some people. Only five feet tall, Chris Carter had dark brown eyes, slightly slanted at the corners, and a broad, flat nose. The most appealing part of his appearance was his wide smile, which came readily to his face.

"You comin', Miss Spencer?" Chris called as he started for the back door with his mother.

"Yes, we'll be along." She waved the group on, then turned to Andrew. "Have you made your decision yet?"

"I thought you wanted me to get to know Chris first."

"Yes, of course. Then we'd better hurry." She started forward.

"Why?" Andrew hung back.

"So we can sit at the same table as Chris. He's very popular."

"Does he know about this job you want to get him?"

A few feet away, Sadie pivoted toward Andrew. "He knows I'm looking for a job for him."

"But not at IFI?"

"I didn't want to get his hopes up."

"His hopes up?"

"His father worked at IFI until he died."

"Who was his father?"

"Harold Carter."

"Harold Carter?" Andrew creased his brow. "Didn't he die a few years back from a heart attack?"

"Yes. He was only forty. Chris took it very hard."

The auditorium door slammed shut, and Sadie realized they were the only ones left. She stared at Andrew, drinking in the sight of him in a three-piece gray pinstripe suit with a dark red tie, a bold statement in his otherwise conservative attire. She'd missed him these past few days and often had found herself daydreaming about their thirty-hour date in New Orleans.

"Then we'd better get to Mitchell's. I want to meet this young man. I won't agree to the pilot program unless I think he has a good chance of employment after graduation. That's only fair to everyone."

"What kind of pizza do you like? I'm buying," Sadie said as they left the auditorium.

"Nonsense. I can—"

"You are my guest, Andrew Knight. It's the least I can do for you, for coming here to present the check in person."

"Canadian bacon. How about you?" Andrew held her car door open for her.

"A supreme with everything on it except anchovies. I'm not big into fish, especially on my pizza."

"Then we agree on something. I'm not either."

"If you don't watch out, before you know it we'll be in complete agreement."

"I doubt that will ever be the case. We look at life entirely differently."

"Ah, but that adds spice to the mix."

"Sometimes too much spice can lead to heartburn."

"At least you know you're alive." Sadie started her engine. "I'll meet you at Mitchell's."

On the short drive, Sadie reflected on what Andrew had said. She'd grown up in a household where her mother had agreed with everything her father said. She often wondered if her mother had an original thought since she'd married. There were times she found herself wanting to stick up for her mother and having to bite her tongue to keep from saying anything. Perhaps her mother and father were very well matched. Or perhaps her mother had discovered it was easier not to disagree. Sadie knew one thing from watching her parents' marriage—she could never be involved with a man who didn't accept her differences. Was there even a man like that?

Sadie pulled into a parking space near the front of the restaurant. Inside Mitchell's, she scanned the tables and saw that Chris and his mother were still alone. While heading toward them, she noticed Andrew enter.

"Mind if we join you?" Sadie asked, aware of Andrew weaving his way through the crowded restaurant toward them.

"Oh, no. It gives me a chance to personally thank Mr. Knight for the generous donation." Amanda Carter removed her purse from a chair so Sadie could sit down.

"Me, too." Chris chimed in as Andrew pulled out the chair next to Sadie and eased into it. "We needed uniforms for ages. Thank you, Mr. Knight." A grin split his face almost ear to ear.

"You're welcome."

"You know what we want, Chris. Do you want to order for us?" Amanda asked, opening her purse for some money.

Chris leaped to his feet. "Sure. Can I have a large soda?"

"No, not so close to your bedtime."

Sadie started to rise. Andrew placed his hand on her arm to still her movements. "I'll order for us. It gives me a chance to talk to Chris."

"Well, then here's—"

"I'm paying."

"But—" Sadie was protesting to a retreating back. She snapped her mouth closed and thought of how heavy-handed her father could be at times, never considering her wishes. Was Andrew like that? Then she realized she was overreacting. Most gentlemen would do exactly what Andrew had done.

"I remember Mr. Knight from when Harold worked at IFI. He'd just been promoted to his new job in human resources, and everyone was glad. They thought he would be fair and willing to try new things. I also heard he works twenty-four seven. How were you able to persuade him to come to the high school tonight?"

Sadie glanced at the man in question and noticed he was talking with Chris. Her student, who had a big grin on his face, laughed and gave Andrew a high five. "It wasn't that difficult. I asked. He accepted," she answered, her gaze still fixed upon Andrew and Chris, deep in conversation.

"Then maybe he isn't immune to a pretty face. At work it was always strictly business with that man, if the rumors are to be believed."

Sadie felt the heat of a blush slowly rise on her face. She remembered Jollie's comments at the bachelor auction and wondered if everyone—at least the women—sat around discussing Andrew Knight. There was an air of vulnerability about him, but he guarded that secret. To the world he presented a confident, controlled facade, which she had glimpsed cracks in.

"I wouldn't know anything about those rumors." Sadie waved to one of her students sitting with her whole family.

"They're coming back to the table. I see Chris has made a new friend. He doesn't know what the word stranger means."

That was one of the things Sadie was counting on. Chris probably knew all fifteen hundred students at the high school, if all the greetings he received in the hallways were any indication.

"Miss Spencer, Mr. Knight is gonna come see us." Chris slipped into his chair.

"When?"

"I told Chris I would try to come see his soccer match next Friday," Andrew said, setting the drink on the table.

Her eyes widened. "You did?"

"He's never been to a soccer game." Chris stopped one of his friends, who was going back to his table. "This is James. He's one of the goalies."

James mumbled something, his eyes downcast.

"Mr. Knight's coming to see us," Chris announced to James and another student going by.

"Only if I can get away," Andrew tried to explain, but Chris had already jumped up from the table and left to spread the word.

Sadie sank her teeth into her lower lip to keep from smiling. Andrew didn't know what to do to stop the rumor of his visit from flying around the restaurant. He started to rise, then shrugged and relaxed in his chair.

"I guess I'd better try to make it."

She decided to give him an out. "If you can't make it, they'll understand. They love playing in front of people, and you're their newest hero."

"Hero?"

Sadie nearly laughed out loud at the stunned expression on Andrew's face. "They've been wanting new uniforms for quite some time. Wait till you see their old ones on Friday. That is, if you can come." She quickly went on to cover the uncomfortable silence. "They've been practicing for the past month with their special partners."

"Special partners?"

"Students in regular education classes. We play unified soccer. Half the team are students who are Special Olympians and the other half are special partners. Everyone has a lot of fun even if we don't always win."

Five minutes later, Chris came to the table. "They just called our numbers. I'll bring our pizzas."

While standing at the counter waiting for his order, Chris saw a group of high school boys come into Mitchell's. He greeted each one with a high five. Chris dragged one of the students to the table.

"Mr. Knight, this is Cal. He's on the team, too. He practices with us."

"Did you forget our pizzas?" his mother asked, shaking her head as though she were used to this from her son.

Chris smiled sheepishly. "Sorry."

Before Cal returned to his friends, he said, "Nice meeting you. Chris is excited about the new uniforms. He said you're buying them for the team."

"Well, not exactly. IFI is," Andrew said, taking a large sip of his iced tea.

"That's great! My dad works for IFI." Cal joined his friends while Chris carried the first pizza to the table, then retrieved the second one.

The aroma of baking bread and sizzling meats that permeated the restaurant made Sadie's mouth water. Her stomach rumbled. The minute Chris placed her pizza between her and Andrew, she scooped up a large piece and took a bite.

"I know pizza is mega calories, but nothing beats it," she said after washing down her food with a sip of her soda.

For the next ten minutes silence prevailed at the table while they all satisfied their hunger. Halfway through her third piece, one of Sadie's students stopped by the table.

"Miss Spencer, I'll see ya tomorrow." The girl threw her arms about Sadie and hugged her. "You're beautiful."

"Thank you, Melissa. You've made my day."

Chris leaned over the table as though imparting a secret. "Melissa always thinks everyone is beautiful. But she's right about you, Miss Spencer."

"If I wasn't blushing before, I'm sure I am now."

"Yep, you're a nice shade of red," Andrew said with a wink. He lifted his glass and downed the rest of his iced tea, his gaze linked to hers the whole time.

She grinned. "Which clashes with my maroon shirt."

"Oh, no, Miss Spencer, you look great. I like what you're wearing." Chris waved to another student across the room. He rose and tossed down his paper napkin. "Mom, I'll be over there."

Chris left, threading his way through the crowded dining room. Sadie chuckled. "And people ask me why I teach students with special needs. They're absolutely great for the ego."

"I'm beginning to get the picture." Andrew watched Chris for a moment before continuing. "Is there anyone he doesn't know?"

"Not at Cimarron High."

"I can attest to that. Our phone is constantly ringing. Thank goodness I don't have a life outside the home or I would never hear from them." Amanda gathered her purse and stood. "I'd better pull Chris away. Tomorrow is a school day, and it will take him at least an hour to calm down after your news, Mr. Knight. Thank you for the donation." Amanda held out her hand, and Andrew shook it.

"I'm glad IFI could help."

While Chris's mother made her way across the restaurant to get her son, Sadie finished her pizza, suddenly not sure what to say to Andrew. She surveyed her few students who were still eating with their families and friends. Their open, guileless faces confirmed her reason for teaching in the first place.

"Because I want this pilot program to work, I want to run this by Mr. Wilson. If we're going to do this project with your school, I want to do it right."

What would her students say if she followed Melissa's lead and threw her arms around Andrew? She refrained from doing that, but she could feel her whole face beaming with a smile.

"Don't say anything. It's not official, Sadie."

"Not a word from this mouth until you tell me I can."

"Now that's an intriguing idea."

"Let me rephrase that. Not a word from this mouth about the project until you tell me I can. Is that better?"

"No, I like it the other way." His eyes danced with a twinkle.

"If I didn't know better, I would think *the* Andrew

Knight is teasing me. I didn't think you had a playful bone in your body.''

"I have my moments. And speaking of time—''

"We were?'' Sadie couldn't help asking, knowing where the conversation was leading.

"I need to leave. I still have some work to do tonight. I'll walk you to your car.''

"You don't have to. This isn't a date.''

"Still, I'll walk you to your car.''

The firmness underlying his words reminded her again of the control the man exhibited. He wasn't used to people denying him anything. He definitely needed his cage rattled.

"Okay,'' she said slowly, trying to decide what to do. "I need to say good-night to my students who are still here.''

"Fine.'' A wariness crept into his voice as he watched her push back her chair.

Sadie made the rounds of her five students and their families left at Mitchell's, refusing to look toward the table where she'd had dinner with Andrew. If she caught his hard gaze, she'd probably lose her nerve to teach him a point.

She held Melissa's baby sister for a few minutes, contorting her face into silly expressions to get the child to laugh. She took an extra moment to go over the plans for the soccer tournament the following week with Kevin's mother. By the time she returned to the table twenty minutes had passed. She expected to see Andrew fuming or gone, but he sat calmly, bent over his paper napkin, writing some notes on it.

"I didn't think you had it in you,'' Sadie said, standing over him.

He peered up, surprised to see her. "What?"

"The patience to wait."

"I have a lot of talents you probably aren't aware of. When you travel as much as I do, you learn real quickly, if you want to keep your sanity intact, ways to occupy your time when you're unexpectedly delayed."

She laughed. "Touché."

He arched one of his dark eyebrows. "Were we having a contest?"

"I think you know very well we were."

In one fluid movement he rose. "Who won?"

"I think we both made our point."

"You don't like someone telling you what to do, and I am capable of going with the flow when I need to. Not such a hopeless case, am I?"

"I never said that." She winked and turned to leave.

Before she had a chance to thrust the restaurant door open, Andrew stepped around her and held it for her. She hurried into the cool night air, glad for its refreshing crispness.

At her car he lounged against the front fender and crossed his arms over his chest. Sadie paused, her hand on the handle, aware she couldn't very well drive away with him leaning against her Honda.

"I thought you had to get back to work."

"I do. I wanted to stop for a moment and—what was it you said? Smell the roses."

"I think you enjoy teasing me."

"It's hard to resist when you make it so much fun."

"I didn't know that word was in your vocabulary."

"You know, if I wasn't such a laid-back kind of guy I would take offense at your constant insistence I don't know how to have a good time."

She almost said, "Prove it," but suppressed the words.

His chuckle floated on the light breeze. "You're too easy to read. I'm just going to have to show you I can have a fun time, like the next guy."

"Oh?" Her doubt drenched that one word.

He shoved away from the fender and straightened, his large presence looming before her and exuding power. "Let's make a deal. If I come to the soccer match, you have to go out with me that evening. I'll show you what I like to do the rare times I do kick back and relax."

"Will you have an answer about the work project by then?"

His chuckles evolved into laughter. "Persistent, aren't you? Yes, I should. What do you say, Sadie? Do you dare find out what I think is fun?"

"I thought the date I bid on was your idea of a fun date."

"Oh, no, far from it. Now, the change in plans to New Orleans was closer to the truth."

Fascinated, against her better judgment, she nodded. "But I have to warn you that I'm usually pretty exhausted after one of these tournaments."

"I'll keep that in mind while planning our date." Andrew gripped the handle and opened her car door. "Till Friday, Sadie."

She slid behind the steering wheel and clasped the cold plastic so tightly her hands ached. What was he up to?

If he hadn't tied it to him coming to the tournament, she could have said no. Who was she kidding? She couldn't say no to his invitation no matter how it was issued. This man intrigued her more than she cared to acknowledge. She was sure if she was around him that could change. After all, he was much too domineering and commanding for her. She'd lived with her father's demands. There was no way she would ever become involved with a man who wouldn't allow her to be herself.

Chapter Six

Sadie didn't have to turn around to know that Andrew had finally arrived at the beginning of the last game of the tournament. She seemed to have a sixth sense when it came to him. She felt his gaze upon her even before she glanced to see him strolling across the field toward her.

In a three-piece navy blue suit, Andrew looked out of place, and yet he didn't. She suspected it wouldn't make any difference what clothes he wore. He had an air of confidence about him that announced to the world he set his own rules, and that wearing business attire to a soccer match was perfectly acceptable.

A roar from the stands pulled Sadie's attention to the game unfolding without her coaching. Kevin dribbled toward the opposing team's goal, came to a halt and swung his foot toward the ball. He missed. An opponent stole the ball and headed toward Chris, Cimarron High's goalie.

"Chris, you can stop it," Sadie shouted, moving down the line toward him. "Cal, set the defense up."

When the Tulsa team made a shot at their goal, Sadie held her breath while Chris dove toward the ball and landed on top of it. The parents and benched teammates stood, yelling their excitement.

Sadie clapped and cheered, pumping her arm into the air. "I knew you could do it."

"If you don't watch out you won't have a voice left." Andrew positioned himself next to her with his hands in his pants' pockets.

"I usually don't. It's a good thing these games are on Friday. It gives me two days to get my voice back. I'm an interactive coach."

"I can see that."

"What I see is that you made it—barely."

"Would you believe that a meeting at work held me up?"

"Yes. Thirty more minutes, and all bets would have been off." Sadie noticed her team had lined up on the field for the kickoff, and she hadn't even realized it. "Go sit down and let me concentrate on the game."

"Do I fluster you, Sadie?"

She rolled her eyes skyward. "You're a distraction—an unwanted distraction."

"I think you wounded my male ego."

"Go." She waved him toward the stands and then focused her attention on the game proceeding without her.

Distraction was an understatement, Sadie decided

at the half as her team was running off the field. Thank goodness they were playing well without the benefit of her coaching, because she couldn't seem to concentrate.

"Get water, everyone," Sadie called to her players. Out of the corner of her eye she saw Andrew strolling toward her. "You all are doing a great job. We're ahead by two goals." *No thanks to me,* she added silently, beads of perspiration popping out on her upper lip.

She removed her white hat and fanned her face. This was worse than the time her parents came to see her coach a game. She felt the pressure weighing her down and wished she had discouraged Andrew from coming. He stopped next to her.

With his usual big grin, Chris approached Andrew. "I'm glad you came. We're winning! Did you see me stop that goal?"

"That was perfect," Andrew said.

At hearing the word perfect, Sadie cringed. "You need to get some water. The game will be starting soon."

"Can I play forward? I want to score."

"Change places with James."

Chris ran off to get some water and sit between two high school girls who had accompanied the team as cheerleaders. Sadie shook her head, amazed at the ease Chris had conversing with anyone. If he got the job at IFI, he would do fine.

"Any word about the work project?" she asked, needing to put business between her and Andrew.

"It's a go. When do you want to start the program?"

"As soon as possible."

"That's what I thought you would say. I need you to meet with the person in charge of the mail room. I cleared a time Monday afternoon. We'll meet with Mrs. Lawson in my office at four o'clock, if that's okay with you."

Thank you, Lord. With Your help this will work. "I'll be there. When can I tell Chris and his mother?"

"When we've worked out the details with Mrs. Lawson."

"But—" She clamped her mouth shut on the protest. She wanted to shout her good news to the whole world, but she would wait.

"For this to work you'll need to sell Mrs. Lawson on the idea."

"Yes, of course. May I ask one more favor?"

"You do know how to push a guy."

"Will you or Mrs. Lawson interview Chris for the job? I want him to experience the whole process, starting with filling out an application."

"I will, but he'll also talk with Mrs. Lawson."

Andrew's gaze strayed to the young man in question, who was smiling at the pretty girl next to him as though he were the cat who had swallowed the canary. "I have to warn you, Mrs. Lawson is rather stern. She runs a tight department and doesn't tolerate any playing around."

"Chris will adjust," Sadie said with more conviction than she felt. Chris always did best with a person who was nurturing and easygoing. She had a lot riding on how well Chris did, but she would never let him know that.

The referee blew his whistle, signaling the start of the second half. Her team lined up, positioned to accept the kickoff.

"Do I have to sit in the stands? I promise I won't say anything to distract you."

She didn't think that was possible, but that wasn't his problem. He couldn't help it if she was attracted to him. "Fine," she answered, and glanced toward him. A mistake, she discovered when her gaze was trapped by the warmth in his eyes and the humor in his expression.

She missed the first few plays of the second half. Forcing herself to look away from Andrew and toward the field, she determinedly ignored the man next to her—for all of ten minutes. When Chris broke loose from the pack with the ball, Andrew's cheers sounded above everyone else's. He headed down the line as Chris headed for the opponent's goal.

"Shoot," Andrew called when Chris had a clear shot on the goal.

The twenty-year-old brought his foot back and sailed the ball through the air. It whizzed by the goalie's head and into the net. Sadie jumped up and down, and before she knew it, she was being crushed against Andrew, whose enthusiasm matched hers.

Then suddenly he realized he held her and she realized she held him. They broke apart. A flush crept up her face. "I—I—" She stammered and couldn't form a coherent sentence. She turned away, shaken and flustered.

"I think I'll sit in the stands," Andrew said, as stunned as she was.

With a quick glance, she saw him settle next to one of her students, Melissa, who proceeded to chatter. It took a few seconds for him to wipe the amazement from his expression and fix on what Melissa was saying to him. Then the team manager, Tina, joined in the conversation. Sadie knew he would be occupied with those two. He would have to focus hard to understand Tina and even then would probably only understand a word or two. His brow was furrowed in concentration.

She relaxed and riveted her full attention on the last few minutes of the game. A member of the Tulsa team dribbled toward James, who crouched low, his arms out to the sides as though he were going to bearhug his opponent. The girl punched the ball past James, who watched it bounce into the net, still perfectly poised. He fell to his knees and bent over. He remained like that even as the teams lined up to kick off. The referee blew his whistle, announcing the game was over.

While everyone formed a line to shake the Tulsa team's hands, Sadie heaved a sigh and walked onto the field to retrieve James. She knelt next to him, placing her hand on his hunched back.

"We won. You need to congratulate the other team on a good game."

"I miss. I miss." James mumbled and pounded the dirt, tears streaming down his face.

Sadie captured his hands and held them, forcing him to look at her. "It's okay. Remember it's not if you win or lose but how you play the game. You played a good game, James." Sadie stood and extended her hand. "Come on. I need to say a few words to the other coach. Will you come with me?"

James sniffed and clasped her hand. "No like goalie."

After talking to the Tulsa coach, Sadie walked with James to the sidelines where the rest of the team was drinking water and high-fiving each other. She searched the crowd for Andrew and found him still sandwiched between Melissa and Tina, both talking to him at the same time, Tina waving her hands as she tried to pantomime what she was trying to tell him. He whipped his attention between the two girls, but Sadie saw the dazed look in his eyes. Taking pity on him, she headed toward them.

"Tina, as our team manager you need to get our practice balls. Melissa, please help her so we can leave right after the awards presentation."

The pair hopped up and hurried to do their jobs. Sadie sat next to Andrew, suddenly tired, her throat parched.

"I think Tina was trying to tell me about going to the ballet in Tulsa."

"She did, last weekend. She tells anyone who will listen. It left quite an impression on her."

"Well, Melissa wasn't going to let her hog the conversation so she started in on telling me about her camping trip last summer.''

"Melissa and Tina are best friends, but they're competitive when it comes to getting someone's full attention. When Tina first came to my class, she didn't speak a word. Now I have a hard time keeping her quiet. I love it, even if I can only understand every third or fourth word.''

"You don't understand her? I was worried maybe it was just me. Melissa didn't seem to have much trouble understanding Tina.''

Sadie laughed. "Yeah, they sometimes complete each other's sentences.''

Andrew rose. "I'll pick you up tonight at six. Wear something casual.''

"Where are we going?''

"It's a secret.''

Sadie pushed to her feet. "You know I don't like surprises or secrets. I thought I made that clear in New Orleans.''

"Yep, crystal clear. But you aren't gonna find out from me. You're just gonna have to wait. I know you have lots of patience. I've seen you with your students.'' His pressed lips and smug expression underscored his intention to keep their destination a secret.

"You're enjoying this way too much,'' Sadie said, starting for the shelter at the park where the awards ceremony would be held.

"Yes, actually I am having fun.'' He fell into step next to her.

"I have to warn you I'm pretty tired.'' When he

didn't say anything, she added, "Your plans don't involve a lot of exertion, do they?"

"Well, that depends on what you call exertion. You'll just have to wait and see." With a cocky smile and a salute, Andrew headed for his car.

Sadie peered at Andrew as he negotiated the streets of Tulsa, amazed that he even owned a pair of jeans, let alone a faded, worn pair that obviously meant he hadn't gone out and bought the jeans that day.

At a stoplight he turned his attention—and charm—on her. His face lit with a smile, and he looked every inch a relaxed man. The classical music playing and the comfortable temperature of the warm autumn night lent further soothing strokes to the evening. Then why was she wound as tight as—

Her eyes grew round as Andrew pulled into the parking lot of an amusement park. The large roller coaster loomed before them, and lots of lights sparkled in the darkening night.

She riveted her gaze to his face. "This is your idea of fun?"

"In some people's books fun and amusement are synonyms."

"But not yours!" Her voice rose, and later—when she was thinking and acting rationally—she would attribute it to exhaustion. She loved amusement parks. He couldn't. It was necessary they didn't have anything else in common. Otherwise, it would be very difficult to fight her attraction to this man. "When was the last time you went to an amusement park?"

He smiled a bit too smugly. "Last summer."

"Last summer! How long did you stay?"

"Several days."

"Really?" She knew Andrew Knight was a complex man, but his answer emphasized it even more.

His eyes gleamed. "Really."

She searched her mind frantically for an explanation that would fit with her image of Andrew. "Why did you go? I thought you never took a vacation."

He pinned her with his penetrating gaze. "It was a business trip."

"I knew it!" Sadie said, relieved that her image was still intact. "That's an unusual place for a business trip."

"Theme parks serve food. It's perfectly logical when you work for a food company."

"Yes, logical," she murmured, the world righting itself. "Back to my original question. When was the last time you were at an amusement park for fun?"

"When I was nine. I used to love to go. I haven't been to one since my family died."

Her heart expanded, and any triumph she felt that she'd figured him out vanished. She shifted so she could face him. "I'm sorry. I didn't mean—"

He pressed his fingers to her lips. "Shh. This is a night of fun. I thought it was about time that I recaptured some of my youth and I couldn't think of anyone I would like better to share it with."

She beamed, her exhaustion completely gone. "Then by all means let's head for the midway. I haven't had cotton candy in ages."

Hand in hand they walked to the ticket booth, and Andrew paid for them to get in. Inside, the scents of popcorn and hot dogs drifted to Sadie as the sounds of bells, clangs and laughter punctuated the air.

"What do you want to ride first?" Andrew asked, looking up and down the long midway.

"You pick. I come to the amusement park at least once a year."

"By yourself?"

"No. Usually with my students. That way I have an excuse for acting like a kid and going on every ride there is."

"Nothing makes you sick?"

She patted her stomach. "Tough as nails. Coated in iron."

"Well, in that case let's do the Ferris wheel first."

From the gleam in his eyes she had expected him to ride the most challenging one first. "Ferris wheel?"

He chuckled. "Don't worry. We'll work our way up. Before the evening is over you'll be thoroughly spun, twisted and twirled until you won't know which way is up or down."

"Promise?"

His chuckle evolved into full laughter. "Yes." He grabbed her hand and tugged her toward the Ferris wheel.

Two hours later, full from eating two hot dogs and one cotton candy washed down with a large soda, Sadie stood next to Andrew staring at the huge roller coaster, known for its thrilling ride.

"This is the last ride. Ready?" Andrew asked, tossing the last of his drink into the trash.

Sadie positioned herself at the end of the line waiting to get on the ride, with Andrew right behind her. "I'm glad we saved the best one for last."

"What I can't figure out is how a woman who loves to go on any ride—some that look as though they defy the laws of nature—can't stand to fly."

"When you figure it out, please let me know. Fears are often irrational. I used to say it was because I have no control when I'm flying, but then I really don't have any control on one of these rides, either."

"Not an ounce."

"So I guess that's not the reason. What are you afraid of?" She shuffled forward when the teenage boy running the ride allowed the people in front of her to sit in the cars.

"Let's go to the back." Andrew steered her through the small crowd and claimed the last car.

After they were secured, the metal bar across their laps, Sadie said, "You haven't answered my question."

"Fire, and there's nothing irrational about that fear."

For a moment Sadie was hurled back to New Orleans. She stood in front of the charred remains of his home, and her heart ached for a little boy who watched his family perish. Saying she was sorry wasn't adequate. She was glad when the roller coaster started, because there was nothing she could say to take away his pain, and she wished there was.

She covered his hand on the bar as the cars chugged upward for the first drop. He linked his fingers through hers, his gaze bound to hers as they reached the top. For a few seconds high above Tulsa with the lights glittering below them, Sadie felt suspended, stopped in time. Andrew leaned toward her and brushed his lips across hers, soft as the warm breeze.

Then the car plunged downward at an alarming speed. But all Sadie could think of was the light feel of his lips against hers. For a few seconds they had been connected on many levels. She wondered in that moment if he had captured her heart.

Thankfully—because she didn't want her emotions to be tangled up with him—the wind rushing by her, the screams of excitement and fear and the sensation of leaving her stomach at the top of the roller coaster brought her back to reality. After that, she experienced the ride, relishing the breeze blowing through her hair, the sudden drops, the exhilarating speed. When the car came to a stop at the end, Sadie closed her eyes for a moment while her pulse quieted.

"I told you I'd tell you when my fourth wish came true. It did," she said, not really thinking clearly, or she wouldn't have admitted it.

"To ride a roller coaster?"

"No." His gaze touched hers, and the feel of his lips feathering across hers replayed in her mind. "I wanted you to kiss me."

For once it seemed Andrew was speechless, surprise dominating his expression.

Sadie quickly stood, her legs shaky. She grasped Andrew to steady herself. "I think my exhaustion is finally catching up with me. Friday night is usually my meltdown night."

"Meltdown night?"

"I go home after school, get takeout from a restaurant and collapse after a long week of teaching. I must confess it's the one night I vegetate in front of the TV. I'm not even sure what I watch half the time. I often wake up at two or three in the morning in my lounger in front of the TV with some awful show on that is only on in the middle of the night."

"Interesting."

"I guess you never do something like that." Sadie walked next to him toward his car, aware of his penetrating regard on her face.

"Can't say that I do. I don't think I've watched television in months."

"What do you usually do on Friday night? We've already established it isn't going to an amusement park."

"Work. I leave IFI about seven or eight, grab something at a fast food place and go home and work some more."

"No dates?"

He stopped at his car and faced her. "Occasionally. I'm here right now, aren't I? How about you? No dates on Friday night?"

"Occasionally. I'm here with you, aren't I?"

"Yes, delightfully so."

She inclined her head. "Thank you."

"About that kiss—"

She covered his lips with her fingertips. "If I hadn't agreed to tell you when my fourth wish happened, you'd never have known. But I'm a woman of my word. No more discussion." *Please,* she silently added.

He looked at her long and hard for a breath-held moment, then opened her door before going around to his side and climbing into the car. "I had a fun evening."

"So did I," she said with relief, glad he was dropping the subject of their brief kiss and her wish. "I didn't think about anything important."

"I have to admit until just a moment ago I didn't think of IFI once," he said with a touch of amazement.

"Now you know it can be done."

He slipped in another classical CD, this time the soothing sounds of Brahms. Sadie settled her head on the cushion. The motion of the car, the warm wrap of darkness, lured her to sleep.

An hour later Andrew shook her awake. "You're home and you have a visitor."

Sadie jerked up and saw her mother sitting on her porch swing and a suitcase next to the front door. "Oh, no. Something must be wrong."

Sadie scrambled from the car before Andrew had a chance to come around and open the door for her. She hurried to the porch, aware that Andrew was behind her, matching her quick steps.

Stunned, Sadie came to a stop in front of her

mother on the swing. "Mom, what's wrong? Why are you here?"

"I've left your dad and I'm moving in with you."

"What happened?" Her stomach knotted.

"He didn't like the dinner I fixed him. He left to eat out and that's when I left him." Her mother fixed her gaze on Andrew. She rose and extended her hand. "I'm Abby Spencer."

"Nice to meet you, Mrs. Spencer. I'm Andrew Knight—a friend of Sadie's."

"Ah, you're the young man she bet on at the auction."

Sadie hadn't thought it possible Andrew could blush, but he did. "Come in, Mom. We need to talk."

"This is my cue to leave. Thanks for the fun evening, Sadie."

"Don't leave on my account. Come in, Mr. Knight, and I'll fix us some coffee. I have a feeling it will be a long night."

That was an understatement, Sadie thought, the knot in her stomach constricting even more.

"Some other time. I have work that I've neglected."

"Thanks for everything. I'll see you at four on Monday." Sadie watched Andrew leave before unlocking her door and waving her mother into her house.

"He seems like a nice young man. Are you two dating?"

"No, Mom."

"Then what were you doing?"

"We're friends. That is all. His company is going to be a work site for one of my students."

"Then it was business tonight?"

Sadie remembered the shared laughter, the brief kiss. "No, we went to the amusement park in Tulsa."

"In my day, that was called a date."

"Mom! Tell me what happened tonight."

"I already did. Your father threw my beef stew out and left. For over thirty years I have cooked and cleaned for that man, and that's how he treats me. He's never done that."

Sadie dug her teeth into her bottom lip to keep from saying what she wanted to. From where she'd stood as a daughter, her father had never treated her mother the way a husband who really loved his wife should. Granted, he might not have thrown her dinner out, but he'd done many things far worse—like ignore her mother, who worked hard to make his home comfortable.

Tears crowded her mother's eyes. She sank onto the couch in the living room. "I know it didn't taste great." She swiped at a lone tear coursing down her cheek. "But I deserve better than that. I—" She hiccupped. "Sadie, I think he's seeing another woman. I can put up with a lot of things, but not that."

Sadie gathered her mother into her arms and held her, stroking her back. "Why do you think he's seeing another woman?"

"Because he's never home anymore. He was supposed to be at the university the other night working late and when I called no one answered his phone in his office. Where was he?'' Her mother leaned back, tears flowing freely down her face. "I know I've put on some weight and I might not be as interested in history as he is, but—'' Her words faded into silence.

"I think you need to talk to Dad about this. There may be a logical explanation for the other night."

"It's not just that. I came in on him yesterday on the phone. He was very secretive and hung up quickly. And just last week I received several calls and no one was on the phone. I've read Ann Landers. I know the signs. What should I do?"

Her mother was asking a woman who was afraid to have a committed relationship with a man, who was afraid she could never fulfill a man's ideal, who would rather be alone than expose her flaws to another. "Why don't you talk with Reverend Littleton? I know he counsels married couples all the time. I also think you need to talk with Dad about your suspicions."

Her mother rubbed at the evidence of her tears. "I'm afraid, Sadie. I'm not brave like you."

"You think I'm brave. Mom, I don't know how to open myself up to a man."

"Maybe Reverend Littleton can help you, too." Her mother clasped her hand and patted it.

"Does Dad know where you are?" Sadie asked, instead of commenting on her mother's suggestion. The minister at her church was a kind older man who was renowned for his counseling, but she couldn't see herself opening up to anyone. It seemed so much safer to keep her face hidden.

"No. I didn't even leave him a note."

"Then at least call and leave a message on the answering machine. He'll worry about where you are."

Her mother harrumphed. "I doubt it."

"Then, Mom, do it for me. You can stay as long as you need."

"I'll leave a message. But if he answers, I'm hanging up."

When her mother rose to walk to the phone, Sadie noticed Abby's hands were shaking. Her heart went out to her mother. Sadie had issues with her father, but she didn't want to see her parents' marriage of thirty-two years break up. Marriage was for a lifetime, and that was why she could never see herself married. She was too scared to trust her heart to someone for the rest of her life.

Chapter Seven

"It's so good to see you, Sadie. Come on in." Andrew held his office door open for her, a pleased look on his face.

As Sadie headed toward him, she wanted to do a victory dance in front of Mrs. Fox, who more than once had refused to let her talk to Andrew. Instead, and to her amazement, Sadie walked into the office at a dignified pace with a gracious expression upon her face.

"How's your mother doing?" Andrew asked while gesturing for Sadie to be seated in a comfortable-looking chair in front of his desk.

"She's staying with me for a while, but at least she and Dad are talking, not always in a calm voice, but talking." Sadie sat, relieved to be off her feet after spending all day standing. It was a rare moment she could sit at her desk as Andrew did and work, not when she had so many students all working on something different. "And they've both finally agreed to see Reverend Littleton. I didn't think Dad would, but last night he told Mom he would go with her tomorrow. Of course, he's only committed to one session and he made sure she knew that." When she saw Andrew's grin, she added, "I'm doing it again, aren't I? Giving you more information than you care to know."

"Nervous?"

"Yes. I want this program to work."

His gaze connected with hers. "So do I. I think it would be good for everyone involved."

The warmth in his expression relaxed her. She leaned back in the chair and drew in a deep, fortifying breath.

"Mrs. Lawson is rarely late for anything. I'm sure she will be here any second."

"Can you tell me a little about her—"

A firm knock sounded on his office door, then it swung open and a tiny woman, no more than five feet tall, with black hair pulled back in a tight bun, entered the room. She covered the distance to the other chair next to Sadie in precise, long strides.

"I'm sorry I'm late. There was a mix-up in the mail room that I had to straighten out before I could leave." Mrs. Lawson sat with her back ramrod straight and her hands folded in her lap.

Sadie looked at the older woman and trembled. She half expected to see frost hanging off her eyelashes. *Lord, show me the way to make this work.*

"Mrs. Lawson, this is Sadie Spencer, the teacher at Cimarron High School I told you about."

Sadie started to offer her hand to the woman, but something in Mrs. Lawson's demeanor stopped her. "It's nice to meet you, Mrs. Lawson." Somehow she got the impression no one called the woman by her first name, not even Andrew.

"I understand that you have a student with mental disabilities you would like to place here in the mail room."

Sadie nodded, her throat dry.

"Can he read?"

"Yes, about third-grade level."

"Can he alphabetize?"

"Yes. I'm been working with him, and he's getting quite good."

"Quite good isn't good enough."

The woman's mouth was pinched into a frown, and Sadie felt all her time and energy had been wasted. How was Chris going to succeed with a boss like her? Again Sadie found herself turning to the Lord for guidance, silently sending a prayer for strength to deal with this new challenge.

She looked Mrs. Lawson directly in the eye and said, "Chris is very capable. He'll make any employer a valuable employee with some on-the-job training."

"When is Chris starting in the mail room?" Mrs. Lawson asked, turning her attention to Andrew as though what Sadie had said was unimportant.

"He'll start next Monday. I'll interview him, then send him to you by one o'clock."

"I understand he'll work half days from twelve to four."

"Yes," Andrew said to Mrs. Lawson.

The older woman glanced away for a few seconds, then returned her attention to Andrew. "And if I have a problem with him, what is the procedure I follow? Do I treat him like the other employees?"

"Yes, but inform me if there's a problem."

Sadie gripped the arms of her chair. Mrs. Lawson's tone underlined the wariness the woman felt toward this arrangement. Chris would be a great ambassador for the work program, but Sadie wasn't sure any student would please Mrs. Lawson.

The woman rose, her back stiff. "Then if that is all, I have a lot of work that needs to be done." As she turned, her gaze fell on Sadie. "It was nice meeting you."

Again her tone negated the meaning behind her words, and Sadie's doubts grew. "Thank you for taking Chris."

Mrs. Lawson nodded curtly and headed for the door. When it clicked shut, Sadie released her pent-up breath in a rush and relaxed her tight grip on the arms of the chair. She flexed her hand to ease her aching fingers.

"Andrew, I don't know if the mail room will work."

"It's a good place for Chris to start. Let's give it a chance."

"Will you let me know if there's a problem? I'll be checking periodically, but Mrs. Lawson might not say anything to me until the problem is unsolvable. I've found that happens sometimes."

"I'll call you if she says anything to me." He leaned forward, resting his elbows on his desk, his gaze intent on her face. "I want this to work."

"Thank you for trying this program." Sadie stood, clutching her purse in front of her. "I'll have Chris here next Monday at twelve for the interview and to fill out the paperwork." She turned to leave.

Andrew pushed to his feet. "Sadie?"

She stopped, peering at him.

He walked from behind his desk. "Mr. Wilson, the president of IFI, is having an informal reception at our Grand Lake lodge for the candidates for the presidency this Saturday night. Will you go with me?"

"You're asking me out on a date?"

The corners of his mouth twitched up. "Yes, that's what it sounds like to me. As I told you, I do occasionally go on dates."

"How informal?"

"Casual attire. It's a barbecue."

"Yes, I'll go."

"I'll pick you up at five." He lounged against the desk, crossing his legs at the ankle. "I probably need to warn you that it will be a working evening. Mr. Wilson is hosting this reception for the board to meet the candidates."

"Am I supposed to be surprised?"

"No, just wanted you to know what you were getting yourself into for the evening."

"In other words, I might not see much of my date."

"I'm the only one not married. It would seem odd if I was the only one who didn't show up with a date for the evening."

"This evening affair is sounding more appealing by the second."

He grinned. "I figure with you I don't have to pretend. You know exactly where my interests lie."

Through a valiant effort, Sadie kept her disappointment from showing on her face. She didn't want a relationship with Andrew, but for some reason being reminded he wasn't interested in a relationship hurt more than she wanted to acknowledge. "Yes, I know. You're after the presidency of IFI. Everything else in your life has been placed on hold."

"Exactly." Pushing himself away from the desk, he escorted her toward the door, his hand lightly touching the small of her back. "I'll see you Saturday."

He walked with her all the way to the elevator. Even through the sweater she wore, she felt the warmth of his fingers on her back. For a fleeting moment she wondered what it would be like to lean on this man for support. He was strong, independent, two qualities she admired in a person. And beneath his tough exterior there beat a soft heart, a quality that endeared him to her.

* * *

"Mom, he's gonna be here any minute. Help! What does casual mean to you?" Sadie held up a pair of jeans and some black pants. "Do I wear this or this?" She thrust each selection out in front of Abby.

Her mother leaned against the doorjamb. "Honey, there are many degrees of casual. What did he say?"

"Informal. That's all. Why didn't I quiz him more about what he meant?" Sadie tossed the jeans onto the discarded clothes stacked haphazardly on her bed. "I probably should go with the black pants. You can dress black up or down. Now, what kind of top should I wear?" She turned to her closet and began rummaging through her clothes.

"I've never seen you this nervous. Is something going on with you and Andrew that I should know about?"

Sadie whirled. "No!"

Her mother quirked a brow.

"Honestly, Mom, we're just friends. That's all."

"And you obsess on what to wear with your friends?"

"This reception is important to Andrew. I wouldn't want to be the cause of any problems for him."

"I see." Her mother folded her arms across her chest, the smug expression on her face saying more than her words.

"What do you think?" Sadie held up a white silk blouse then a leopard print shirt. "Which one?"

"The white."

"Yeah, the other makes too bold a statement. I

need to play it low-key. This is Andrew's show. I certainly don't want to draw attention to myself.''

"You should never do that.''

Sadie paused in tossing the leopard print blouse on the growing pile of clothes and eyed her mother. ''You're enjoying this.''

"Yep. I rarely get to see you falling apart over something as minor as two friends going to a reception. Now if this had been a date, I could understand.''

Sadie put her hands on her hips, the leopard print blouse bunched up in her fist. ''This is not a date.''

Her mother straightened from the doorjamb. ''No, dear.''

Sadie started to protest some more when the doorbell sounded.

She gasped. ''I'm gonna be late.''

"I'll entertain Mr. Knight while you finish getting dressed.''

"Mom, don't say—'' Sadie didn't complete her sentence because her mother had disappeared down the hall.

Sadie listened while her mother let Andrew into the house with a cheerful greeting. Sadie leaned her head into the hallway, conscious of the fact she wasn't completely dressed, and tried to hear his reply. They had obviously walked into the living room, and the sound of their voices was too muffled for her to understand what was being said. That prompted Sadie to hurry and throw on her clothes.

No telling what her mother would say to Andrew.

There were times she could have an impish streak. Sadie remembered once in high school her mother regaling her date about some of her antics while she was growing up. She had come into the room just in time to stop her mother from pulling out the albums and showing him pictures of her as a baby in less than appealing snapshots.

Ten minutes later Sadie appeared in the living room, ready to yank any albums out of her mother's grasp. She hoped her French braid didn't have too many hairs sticking out and that her lipstick was on straight. Glancing at her clothes, she was pleased to see that at least she looked all right even if inside she felt less than together.

Sadie rushed forward. "Sorry I'm late."

Andrew lifted his head and snared her gaze with his assessing one. "The wait was worth it."

She noted his tan slacks and black polo shirt and breathed a sigh of relief. His idea of casual was the same as hers. "Ready?"

Andrew rose, saying to her mother, "Thank you for the invitation to Thanksgiving dinner, but I'd hate to intrude on your family time."

"Nonsense. It will be a small gathering this year so you're more than welcome. I hate to hear of anyone spending Thanksgiving alone. It's meant to be spent with family—and friends." Her mother winked at Sadie.

She nearly choked.

"Don't you think so, Sadie?"

Her mother looked at her with such innocence in her eyes that Sadie could only nod her agreement.

"You see. Even Sadie feels you shouldn't spend Thanksgiving alone."

"Then it's a date. Thank you for inviting me."

Behind Andrew her mother smirked. "Yes, it's a date."

Sadie stifled her moan, but she knew she would have to talk with her mother tomorrow about trying to matchmake, because that was what she was doing. She was clearly going to have to define friendship for her mother.

"We'd better get going. I wouldn't want you to be late for the reception." Sadie grasped Andrew's hand and practically hauled him toward the front door.

When they stepped outside, the autumn air caressed her cheeks, cooling the heat that suffused her. She was thankful beads of sweat hadn't popped out on her forehead and run down her face to ruin what little makeup she had on.

"If you don't want to come to Thanksgiving dinner, Andrew, you don't have to."

At the car he opened her door, his gaze trapping her. "Do you want me to?"

The intensity in his regard wiped any rational thought from her mind.

"I meant it when I said I didn't want to intrude, Sadie."

The vulnerability she occasionally glimpsed in him surfaced for a brief second. She covered his hand on the door and said, "You could never intrude. I would love to have you spend Thanksgiving with my mother and me.''

''Not your father?''

She tilted her head to the side and thought about that. ''You know, Mom hasn't said anything about that. He might be there. Their counseling session with Reverend Littleton wasn't a rousing success, but at least they're talking.''

''That's good.''

Sadie climbed into his silver Lexus and watched as he rounded the front and slid into his seat. ''My question to you is will you mind coming to dinner if my father is there? The atmosphere may not be very relaxed.'' Sadie refrained from telling Andrew it rarely was when she was with her father. She had told Andrew more about her life than she usually said to anyone, which was a surprise in itself.

''Do you know what I was going to do Thanksgiving?''

''Work?''

''You got it. I was going to go into IFI and work on some reports. There are always reports that need doing.'' He peered at her through a half shuttered gaze. ''My dinner that evening would have consisted of a frozen TV dinner of turkey.''

''Not very appetizing.''

''No, but that's my idea of Thanksgiving if I don't go to Ruth and Darrell's.''

''Why aren't you this year?''

One corner of his mouth lifted in a self-mocking grin. ''Not enough time.''

A dull ache pierced her heart. "Is it all worth it to you?"

"Sadie, I don't know anything else but work, so I have to say yes."

"You don't have to say or do anything if you don't want to."

"That's a pretty naive way to look at life." He started the car and pulled out of the driveway.

"I've never considered myself naive."

"Don't you do things that must be done?"

"Well, yes. Everyone does at some time in his life, but people do make their own choices, you included."

"Exactly. I choose to work. I find comfort in work."

"Because it doesn't require an emotional commitment?"

He sucked in a deep breath. "You do know how to hit below the belt. But then maybe that's because we are alike."

"I know how to commit emotionally. I do to my students."

"Not the same thing as a relationship with a man. You know why I won't commit. Why won't you?"

"Haven't found Mr. Right," she quipped.

"Are you looking?"

"Do you want to be a candidate?" she asked, hoping to shut this conversation down quickly.

"Touché. I'll be quiet. That's what you want."

For the next forty-five minutes silence reigned in the car while the landscape sped past. Sadie was glad for the reprieve. She felt emotionally overloaded from their brief conversation. He had a way of getting past her defenses. She was constantly finding herself having to shore them up when she was around him.

When Andrew pulled into a gated driveway that led to the lake, she noticed his demeanor change. A new tension hung in the air, as though he were preparing to do battle. She could almost see him running through a list of tasks in his head.

"Is there anything I should know, do?" she asked, wishing she could ease his burden.

"No, just be yourself."

"Are you sure about that?" Laughter tinged her words.

He quirked a brow at her. "Should I be worried?"

"No, I'll be on my best behavior. Promise. I would never do anything to ruin your chances of becoming president."

"Now I am worried."

But the expression on his face belied his statement. His features relaxed into an easy grin, and he took her hand as they approached the front door. Her impression of IFI's cabin on Grand Lake was one of a sprawling structure of glass and rustic wood that blended with the surrounding water and woods. The only things out of place were the expensive cars that lined the circular drive, underscoring the purpose of the evening's reception. Tension whipped down her as they waited for someone to open the front door.

When she stepped into the foyer, she felt drawn to the panoramic view from the floor-to-ceiling windows in the living room, which overlooked the lake. The setting sun tinted the water a rosy hue while the color-ful fall leaves on the trees along the shoreline danced in the light breeze. The beautiful vista reminded Sadie of the power in God's creation, in His love. That thought brought peace to her, and she knew every-thing would be all right this evening. She discarded her tension like an unwanted cloak, determined to en-joy herself even if she felt out of her element.

Taking her elbow, Andrew directed her to a small group near the floor-to-ceiling windows. "I want you to meet Lawrence Wilson, the president of IFI. This is Sadie Spencer."

She shook Mr. Wilson's hand. "It's nice to meet you. This place is beautiful."

"I like to entertain here. A much more relaxing environment."

Andrew went around the group, introducing her to the other two candidates for the presidency and their wives. Charles Benson and his wife, Elizabeth, greeted her with smiles and a warmth Sadie found herself responding to. The Edgars, Stephen and Linda, were more formal but nice.

When another man and his wife entered, Lawrence Wilson said, "Now that everyone is here, I have an announcement to make."

The room quieted, and people turned toward him, waiting for him to continue. Andrew enclosed her hand within his, his arm touching hers.

"As you probably all know, since there seem to be no secrets at IFI, I'm retiring next year. What you don't know is that I'm retiring earlier than you think.

I will be stepping down in six months instead of nine, and I've gathered here tonight the three men I think are capable of running IFI after I'm gone.'' Lawrence gestured to each man as he introduced them.

Andrew's hand tightened when his name was announced. She felt his tension as though it were a part of her.

''Over the next few months the board and myself will be taking a careful look at each man to determine who will be the best one to run IFI in the twenty-first century. Good luck.''

Sadie felt as though she were at a horse race, watching the colts contend for the purse. After that announcement the room buzzed with noise as everyone began to talk at the same time—except Andrew, who remained unusually quiet next to her.

He scanned the people and leaned toward her to whisper, ''Let the games begin.''

She smiled. ''I was thinking more along the lines of a horse race.''

He tipped his head back and laughed. ''I've been called many things but never a horse.'' His gaze was riveted to hers. ''Thanks, Sadie, for making me laugh. I needed that.'' His stance relaxed, his grip on her hand a loose connection. ''I guess I'd better start making my rounds.''

''I think I'll escape outside to the deck.''

''Already? The evening's only begun.''

''But the sun is setting, and the sky is beautiful. Later I won't be able to see a thing from the deck.''

''True. Want me to come with you?''

''That would amount to stumbling at the starting gate. No, you need to woo some board members.''

Sadie watched Andrew weave his way through the small crowd, stopping to converse with several people. Mostly she noticed he listened intently to what the others were saying, interjecting a comment when necessary. Any tension he felt wasn't evident, and Sadie thought he was in his element, much as she was teaching her students.

She slipped outside, smiling at several people who were also taking time to absorb the beauty of the sunset slanting across the waters below. The scent of meat roasting on a grill and the sound of water lapping against the shore drifted to Sadie. She wished she could bottle this moment. The breeze rustled the leaves of the maple and oak trees. She shivered in the darkening light, hugging herself.

''Cold?''

She whirled, surprised that Andrew was standing behind her holding a sweater for her.

''I borrowed Mrs. Wilson's sweater. I thought you might be getting cold.''

''But you're supposed to be in there wooing the powers that be.''

He moved close and draped the sweater over her shoulders. ''I have plenty of time to woo. Besides, if my hard work and record don't get me the presidency, then I don't deserve it. I didn't want you to enjoy the sunset by yourself.''

She laid her hand on his forehead. ''What did you do with Andrew Knight?''

He chuckled. "Nothing. He's in here somewhere."

She turned and noticed that the sun had sunk below the trees. "Oh, it's gone. You missed it."

"That's okay." Andrew gripped the railing, leaning into it and slanting a look at her. "Tell me about it. I'd rather see it through your eyes, anyway."

"I—" She couldn't think of a thing to say to that statement.

"Sadie Spencer, don't tell me you're speechless. That's got to be a first."

"You're getting awfully good at teasing me."

The smile that touched his mouth went to her heart. "Yes, you have a gift of bringing that out in a person."

"I think that was a compliment. Thank you."

"It was. You were perfect to bring tonight."

Perfect. There was that word again. She hated it. What would happen when Andrew discovered all her flaws?

The urge to pace Andrew's outer office was strong, but Sadie remained seated next to Chris, her hands gripping her purse as though any second someone was going to dash into the room and snatch it away. Thankfully Chris was flipping through a magazine, oblivious to the turmoil churning in her stomach.

She heard footsteps approaching and glanced up to see Andrew hurrying into the office. He threw her a grin before turning to his secretary and giving her a stack of papers.

"I need these to go out immediately." He snagged

Sadie's gaze and nodded toward his office. "Give me a few minutes. I have to make a quick phone call."

After Andrew disappeared into his office, Sadie took the magazine from Chris and replaced it on the coffee table. "I want you to do this by yourself. I know you think Mr. Knight is a friend, but Chris, when you are at work, remember you greet him with a handshake, not a hug."

"I remember, Miss Spencer."

"Speak slowly and clearly. Don't mumble."

"Why aren't you coming?"

"Because this is something you need to do by yourself. I'll be right out here when you're through."

Andrew opened his door and motioned for them to come inside. Chris stood and walked toward him. "You aren't joining us?"

Sadie shook her head and watched her student enter Andrew's office. For a second her heart stopped beating. This was so important to Chris and to her. She closed her eyes and turned to the One who gave her strength. *Heavenly Father, watch over Chris and be with him. Help him through the interview and the first days on the job. Please help Mrs. Lawson to understand the worthiness of an employee like Chris.*

Fifteen minutes later Sadie had scanned the three magazines on the coffee table and was trying to decide how to occupy her time until Chris was finished. She pushed to her feet and started to walk down the hall to the water fountain when the door to Andrew's office opened and Chris came out with Andrew behind him. Chris grinned from ear to ear.

"You should see how high up we are," Chris exclaimed. "I can see the river from his window."

Sadie suppressed a moan, realizing Chris would never lose his enthusiasm for the small things. "How did everything go?" Her gaze skipped from Chris to Andrew.

"I'm taking him downstairs to meet Mrs. Lawson right now. Would you like to come along?"

Sadie agreed. She followed the pair to the elevator. She wanted to pull Andrew to the side and find out how well Chris did, but she didn't.

"This goes fast," Chris said as the elevator came to a halt on the ground floor.

When they entered the mail room, Sadie noticed everyone was at work. The only sounds were the shuffling of paper and the copy machine running. Chris paused for a moment to survey his new work area. A young man looked up, and Chris grinned and waved at him.

"Come on. Mrs. Lawson's office is this way." Andrew motioned to a closed door with a large window next to it that afforded Mrs. Lawson a view of the mail room.

Again Sadie's reservations surfaced. This would work if the environment was conducive to Chris. She worried about the extra-tight rein Mrs. Lawson seemed to have on the people who worked for her. How would Chris fare when he was so openly friendly and social? Sadie threw a glance over her shoulder at the workers in the room going about their jobs. Her doubts multiplied.

Inside Mrs. Lawson's office Chris sat between Sadie and Andrew while the older woman perused his application. A tiny frown knitted her brow.

Sadie's chest tightened with each breath she dragged in. She flexed her hands, then gripped the arms of the chair and waited for the woman to say something.

Mrs. Lawson looked at Chris. "You will have to clock in and out every day. I will show you where when we leave here. You will have a fifteen minute break at two. If you don't understand something, ask for help. I will have you work with Bert until you learn the job. You'll be delivering and picking up mail as well as sorting it. Do you understand your duties?"

Chris nodded, a big grin on his face.

Andrew rose. "If you don't have any questions for Miss Spencer or me, we'll be leaving then."

"Who'll be picking him up?" Mrs. Lawson asked, standing, too.

"I will, this first day, with his mother. After that his mother will. Today we'll come up with a place for Chris to be when she comes."

"I suggest the lobby."

"Of course." Sadie got the distinct feeling the woman didn't want anyone disrupting her routine in the mail room.

When Mrs. Lawson didn't say anything else, Andrew opened the door and waited for Sadie to leave first. She hated walking away from Chris. Chewing on her bottom lip, she gave Chris one last glance before exiting.

In the lobby Andrew faced her. "It will work out. Mrs. Lawson comes across as being stern and inflexible, but she does a good job running her department."

"But how happy are her employees?"

"I don't receive any complaints. She'll make sure that Chris is trained properly in his job. Will you trust me on this one?"

She nodded. "You know IFI better than I do. I guess I just feel like a mother hen."

"Chris did fine in the interview with me, and he'll do fine with Mrs. Lawson." He began walking her toward the doors that led outside. "What time do you want me to come on Thanksgiving?"

"My father will be there. Mom asked him, and he agreed."

Andrew halted a few feet from the door. "Does that make a difference in me coming or not?"

"No, I just wanted to warn you. My father can be difficult at times."

"And yet you're upset about your mother walking out on your father."

"It seems my feelings concerning my father are all tangled up."

"I don't have to come. I always have work to do here."

She grasped his arm. "I want you to come. I only wanted to warn you about what you might be getting yourself mixed up in. Come around twelve."

"You're going to have turkey and all the trimmings?"

"Yes."

"Then I'll be there. It's not that often I get a home-cooked meal."

Her mouth quirked up. "Then you'll have something to be thankful for."

As she left the building, she sensed Andrew watching her, but she didn't glance back. For the first time in a long while, she was looking forward to Thanksgiving Day. She tucked that knowledge away to examine later when she was alone and had time to reflect.

Chapter Eight

"How do I look?" Abby stood in the doorway of the kitchen and spun around. Her silk peach dress fell in soft waves about her knees.

Sadie noted she was wearing high heels and hose. Since Sadie could remember, her father had insisted they all dress up for Thanksgiving, giving the day a formal touch. "Mom, you look fine. You always do." She went back to sautéing the onions and celery for the dressing.

"Here, let me do that while you get dressed." Her mother took the wooden spoon from Sadie.

"You don't think I'm dressed?" she asked with a laugh, gesturing at the old pair of sweats she had on with evidence of the day's cooking spattered on it.

"While I think you're cute dusted with flour and who knows what, I think if you want to impress that young man you might want to change."

Sadie frowned. "I'm not trying to impress Andrew."

"Then what was that scene a few weeks ago when you were trying to decide what to wear on your date?"

"Mom," Sadie said with a deep sigh, "I was trying to impress the people he works for. IFI can become a valuable workplace for my students."

"Of course, dear." Abby focused her attention on the skillet.

Sadie stared at her for a moment, then sighed again and left the kitchen, realizing she would never convince her mother Andrew was just a friend. For years her mother had tried to get her married, even fixing her up with blind dates. After the third disastrous one Sadie had put a stop to the blind dates.

Nevertheless Sadie was determined to prove a point to her mother. She pulled out a pair of black jeans and a red turtleneck sweater. She wanted to set an informal and casual tone for the afternoon, and she would start with what she wore.

As she brushed her long hair, deciding to leave it loose, she heard the doorbell ring. "I'll get it." She hurried to answer the door. Since her father wasn't due for another hour, Andrew must be a few minutes early.

When she swung it open, her smile faltered. Her father stood on her porch, dressed in a suit. "You're early." It was all she could think to say.

"Yes, I am." He moved past her into the house. "I see you aren't ready yet."

Peering at her attire, she bit on the inside of her cheek, a coldness embedded deep inside her. "I decided to go casual this Thanksgiving."

"Does your mother know?"

"Know what?" Abby came into the foyer, wiping her hands on her apron.

Her father waved his arm toward Sadie.

With a glance from Sadie to Robert, her mother straightened her shoulders and said, "Since this is her house, she sets the tone."

Shock flared in his eyes. "Very well." He continued into the living room.

The bell rang again. Sadie quickly answered the door, glad to have something to do. She forced herself to smile as she greeted Andrew. She was glad to see him, but she didn't know if his coming to dinner was a good idea.

His gaze skimmed the length of her. "You look beautiful."

She blushed under his intent look, any chill she felt gone. "Thank you. You don't look half bad yourself." She took in his attire, black pants and turtleneck with a tan and black sweater.

"Thank you, ma'am. Now that we have the pleasantries out of the way, what's for dinner?"

"I'll give you three guesses, and if you don't get it on the first try, I'll have to tell my mother to forget what I said about you."

Andrew stepped closer, the intensity in his gaze sharpening. "And what was that?"

He was so near that Sadie felt surrounded by him.

Tilting her chin up, she licked her lips and said, "That you were a very smart man."

His eyes glittered. "I'm curious."

"I thought I was the only one around here allowed to get curious."

"Nope." He shook his head slowly. "Why were you and your mother talking about me?"

"Now if I told you everything, that would be way too easy and dull." She spun to go into the living room.

Andrew captured her arm and halted her movement. He spoke into her ear, his breath feathering her neck. "There's nothing wrong with easy and dull."

"Oh, yes, there is, Mr. Knight. As you well know, there's nothing wrong with hard work if something is worth it."

"I'll have to remember that when I'm working late at night. But frankly, Miss Spencer, I can't believe I heard those words from your lips."

"My motto is to expect the unexpected."

She heard her father's raised voice coming from the living room and tensed, the imp inside her vanishing. Suddenly she was reminded of the day to come. There would be nothing easy or dull about this Thanksgiving.

"Let me introduce you to my father, then I need to finish putting the dinner together."

"Can I help?"

She flashed him a smile. "Chicken. Afraid to be alone with my parents?"

"I was hoping to sample some of the food before

it made it to the table.'' He glanced away then at her, a sheepish look on his face. ''I forgot to eat breakfast.''

She placed her hands on her hips. ''Where were you before coming here? This is a holiday, Andrew Knight.''

He hung his head. ''Guilty. I was at work. I just had one report to get out.''

''Tsk tsk. You are a hopeless case, but I'll take pity on you and let you help me in the kitchen. You're familiar with what you do in a kitchen, aren't you?''

''I can microwave a dinner and open a can and heat it on the stove.''

''I'm impressed.''

''Come on. Introduce me to your father before I have no ego left.''

Sadie moved into the living room with Andrew at her side. Her parents were seated on the couch, arguing. Her mother saw Sadie and clamped her mouth shut. Her father twisted to stare at Sadie and Andrew, clearly not happy to be interrupted.

''Dad, I want you to meet Andrew Knight. Andrew, this is my father, Robert Spencer.''

The two men shook hands and retreated to their respective corners, sizing each other up. Sadie wanted to squirm but held herself straight, waiting for something to happen.

''It's a pleasure to meet you finally, Mr. Spencer.''

''I didn't realize we were having a guest for dinner.''

Sadie shot her mother a glare. "You were supposed to tell Dad."

"I forgot." She shrugged. "Other things on my mind. Did I tell you all I have applied for a job at the university?"

"A job! Doing what?" Robert asked, surprise and anger lacing his words.

"I'm going to work in the library. I love books and I decided it was time for me to do something I love."

Sadie tugged on Andrew's arm and pulled him toward the kitchen. As the door closed behind them, she could hear her father demand her mother quit.

"I'm sorry. My mother doesn't always have the best timing."

"I think your mother has perfect timing."

Sadie stared at Andrew for a moment. "I suppose you're right. That's a piece of news she probably didn't want to tell him. At least with us here my father will temper his response." She went to the stove and removed the skillet. After pouring the onions and celery into a large mixing bowl, she added the other ingredients for the dressing.

"It does seem most unusual that Mom would get a job now after all these years of not working. I always thought she liked staying home and taking care of the family."

"Maybe she needed more." Andrew scanned the kitchen. "What can I do to help?"

"Sit over there."

"And?"

"And nothing. I don't have time to teach a novice."

"I'm a quick learner."

"Don't worry. I'll let you sample some of the food. I'll even let you carve the turkey—that is, if you know how to."

Andrew puffed out his chest. "I know how to."

"Really?"

"Well, how hard can it be? You take a big knife and cut the meat off."

"Have you ever done it?"

"No, but I'm sure I can manage."

"On second thought, you sit there and keep me company. I'll carve the turkey."

He placed his hand over his heart. "Oh, you've wounded my ego again."

Sadie opened the oven and checked on the turkey, its aroma filling the kitchen. After placing the casserole dish with the dressing inside, she closed the door and started for the refrigerator.

"Will we get to sample any of that baking you like to do?"

"I made some rolls and a pecan pie. Is that enough for you?" She rummaged in the refrigerator, looking for the ingredients for a salad.

"It is for me. What about you and your parents?"

Sadie popped her head up and slanted a look toward Andrew, who sat comfortably at her kitchen table with a wide grin on his face.

He winked. "I do believe I'm getting the hang of this teasing."

"I'll just have to invite you to one of my parties when I clean out my freezer."

"Promise?"

Suddenly she realized what she had said, implying their personal relationship would go beyond today. She straightened, then dragged out spinach and lettuce. "Yes, the next one I have, which—" she swung the freezer door open to reveal a stuffed compartment "—won't be long. I don't know what I'm going to do about leftovers."

"I'll try to eat more than my share. That ought to help you out."

"Mr. Knight, you are so obliging. Whatever did I do before I knew you?"

"I don't know, but I'm glad I could be of help." He surged to his feet. "And speaking of help. I can wash lettuce and spinach. That doesn't require a culinary degree."

Sadie handed the items to him, then went to the refrigerator to retrieve the rest of the salad ingredients. Seeing Andrew standing at her sink rinsing the lettuce gave her a moment of pause. He looked so right in her kitchen, as though he belonged. For a few seconds she fantasized what it would be like if they had a relationship that was more than friendship. Then she remembered the struggles her parents were going through. She remembered where Andrew had been before he had come to her house for dinner— work, which was where he spent most of his waking time. She shook the fantasy from her mind and set the rest of the salad fixings on the counter.

* * *

Seated at the dining room table, Sadie took her parents' hands and bowed her head. "Dear Heavenly Father, please bless this food and each person at this table. This is a time for thanksgiving, and we have much to be thankful for. Watch over the less fortunate and be with us in our time of need. In the name of Jesus Christ, amen."

Lifting her head, she caught Andrew staring at her from across the table. She realized in that moment she was very glad he was spending Thanksgiving with her. The dread she usually experienced mellowed as his gaze took her in.

"I would have carved the turkey, Sadie." Robert Spencer cut into the silence while forking several pieces of the meat onto his plate.

"That's okay, Dad. I wanted to give Andrew a lesson on how to, and besides, this is my first time to cook Thanksgiving dinner for you all." Sadie thought of the time she and Andrew had spent alone in the kitchen while she finished the meal preparation. His presence would make the next few hours bearable.

"Yes, well, we should have been eating at home. That's how we've always done it."

Her stomach constricted into a huge knot. Sadie gripped the serving spoon for the broccoli casserole, her chest expanding with a deep breath. "Maybe it's time to start a new tradition." After taking some of the vegetable, she passed it to her mother, not sure she would be able to eat it.

"Perhaps when you marry might be a better time to start a new tradition."

Sadie was so close to blurting, "If your marriage is any indication of what it's like, then I want nothing to do with marriage." But she kept her mouth shut, her teeth digging into her lower lip while she took the platter of turkey from her father.

"I understand from Sadie, sir, that you're a history professor at the college. What area is your specialty?"

"Nineteenth-century Europe."

"History was one of my favorite subjects in school," Andrew said, taking a sip of iced tea.

Surprised at that bit of information, Sadie said, "I would have thought something like math would have been."

A smile slowly curved Andrew's mouth. "No. To better understand today, you need to understand yesterday."

"My thoughts exactly." Her father tore off a piece of his roll and popped it into his mouth. "I wish more young people felt like you do."

Sadie refused to look at her father. She heard disappointment in his voice. He'd wanted her to go through the graduate program in history and follow in his footsteps, teaching at the college level. He never stopped letting her know she'd let him down.

"Of course, I feel people must do what's important for them," Andrew continued, his silent support conveyed by the expression in his eyes, directed solely at her. "There are many things important in this world. Thankfully there are people like Sadie who love to teach our children. I couldn't do it, but I know we need good teachers like her."

"Right you are, Andrew," her mother said, patting Sadie's hand. "Robert, did I tell you that Sadie was named teacher of the year at Cimarron High School? She'll be competing with others from the elementary and middle schools for teacher of the year for the whole district. She just found out yesterday."

"That's wonderful." Andrew lifted his glass. "Here's to the best."

"Yes, the best," her mother said, raising her iced tea and clicking Sadie's glass.

Sadie turned her attention to her father, almost afraid to see the expression on his face.

"When will you know?" he asked, cutting his turkey into bite size pieces.

"After the new year there'll be a dinner to introduce the individual schools' teachers of the year, and then they'll announce the district one at that time. That person will go on to the state competition."

"Let me know what happens." Her father forked a piece of meat into his mouth.

Okay, Sadie. What did you expect? A twenty-one-gun salute? "I will," she murmured, her stomach so tight she didn't think she could eat another bite. Even if she won the teacher of the year for the whole country, she doubted it would be enough for her father. That thought caused her spirits to plummet.

"Personally I don't know how you do it."

Andrew's voice pulled her gaze to him. The look of admiration on his face sent her heart beating rapidly. He smiled at her, a gesture that suddenly seemed to wipe everything from her mind but him.

"I've seen you with your students, and you're amazing. If their opinion counts for anything, you'll win hands down."

"I agree, Andrew," her mother said. "She devotes a lot of time to her students."

Sadie glowed under their praise, trying to dismiss the fact that her father said nothing. She knew he thought she wasted her time working with students with special needs. She didn't think she would ever be able to change his mind. Where she saw loving, giving students who had every right to a full, productive life, her father saw students who would never be complete, contributing members of society.

"I don't care who wins in January. It is an honor to have my daughter representing the high school. Andrew, would you like any more dressing?" Her mother held up the bowl.

He shook his head. "I'm stuffed. This was delicious, Mrs. Spencer."

"Oh, please call me Abby, and I didn't do much. Sadie was up at five this morning getting the turkey ready to go into the oven. I mostly watched this time. It was nice. I don't get to do that often. This was certainly a treat."

Suddenly silence blanketed the room, each person intent on moving food around on the plate. Sadie searched her mind for a safe topic that would put an end to the discomfort at the table. Her mind went blank.

"Dr. Spencer, I understand you write books. Are you working on one right now?" Andrew asked.

In that moment Sadie could have kissed him. Her father's favorite subject was the books he wrote. She forced herself to eat a bite of dressing, waiting to see what her father would reply.

"I'm nearly finished with a biography of Prince Albert. I've spent more time on him than I usually do. I wanted to do justice to the man behind the throne." Her father launched into a discussion about how much influence and power Prince Albert had as the husband of Queen Victoria.

Sadie breathed deeply the rich aromas of the foods about her and relaxed in her chair. With Andrew asking pertinent questions the conversation flowed between him and her father as though this were a normal dinner, not one rife with tension. She observed the ease with which Andrew conversed with her father, the great detail of knowledge he had in a field where her father was an expert.

When there was a lull in the conversation, Sadie rose. "Would anyone like a piece of pecan pie with vanilla ice cream?"

Andrew chuckled. "This from a woman who prides herself on eating well-balanced meals."

"I never said I didn't indulge in tempting desserts from time to time. Remember all those things I bake. Not all of them are oat bran muffins."

"Come to think of it, not many were."

"Have you been invited yet to one of her parties when she empties out her freezer?" Her mother stood, too, and started gathering dishes.

"Not yet, but she has promised to invite me to the next one."

The twinkle in Andrew's eyes melted Sadie's tension completely. "Okay, I don't normally plan one of these parties more than a day in advance, but how about this Saturday night? I need to clear the freezer out. Christmas is just around the corner."

"You're on."

"I've seen what's in her freezer. You're in for a treat."

"Mom. Dad. Do you want to join us?" Sadie stacked the plates to carry into the kitchen.

"Oh, no, dear. Your dad and I have the Henderson party to go to."

Her father's eyes widened. "I thought you said you couldn't make—"

"I've changed my mind. If we're going to work out our problems, we'll need to spend some time together." Her mother marched into the kitchen with her hands full of dirty dishes.

"Any pie?" Sadie asked, realizing her mother's real motive.

Andrew scooted back his chair. "I need to walk some of this delicious food off before I indulge."

Her mother entered the dining room. "Andrew, that's a good idea. Why don't you two go for a walk while your father and I clean up? That's the least we can do, since you prepared the dinner."

Her father's eyes grew rounder. He rarely stepped into the kitchen unless it was to eat, certainly never to clean up. Sadie decided to take her mother up on her offer.

"Yes, I think I will." Sadie hurried into the kitchen and put her stack of dishes on the counter.

When she came into the dining room, she noticed an uneasy silence had fallen again. She grabbed Andrew's hand and started for the front door, snatching a sweater as she left.

Outside she paused on her porch and drew in deep breaths of the cool fall air, perfumed with the scent of burning wood. The sky was cobalt blue with not a cloud anywhere. She tilted her face to the sun and relished its warm rays.

"I doubt you've ever had a Thanksgiving like this one," she said when she felt Andrew's probing gaze on her.

"No, but then I don't usually spend Thanksgiving with a family."

"Not Darrell and Ruth's?"

"When I can get away for a couple of days."

"Which isn't that often."

"Not in the past few years." Andrew began walking.

Sadie fell into step next to him, and his strides shortened to accommodate her. "I'm sorry. My father can be difficult at times."

Andrew slid a smile toward her. "Actually I enjoyed our conversation about Prince Albert. As I said, I like history."

"Then you and my dad have something in common."

"You don't like history?"

"Well, yes, I do."

"Then you and I have something in common."

The idea they had more things in common than she thought nonplussed her, causing her step to slow. Andrew went a few feet in front of her, stopped and turned toward her.

"Is that so hard to imagine, Sadie?"

"That we have things in common? No, I guess not. It's just that you and I live our lives so differently."

"Do we?" He held his hand out for her to take. "I think we live our lives very much the same—all or nothing. I've seen you with your students, and you throw yourself completely into it."

The warmth of his fingers on hers was like the rays of the sun on her face. She savored the feel, realizing somewhere that day she had given up the notion that they were just friends. It was more than that, at least on her part, and that thought scared her more than a confrontation with her father.

They continued their walk, their hands linked. Andrew steered them toward the park.

"If you're going to be a good teacher, you have to give a part of yourself to your students."

"And if I'm going to be a good executive, I have to give a part of myself to the job and the people who work for me."

"But I can draw the line between work and pleasure."

Andrew took a few more steps without saying a

word, then he said, "Tell me about your relationship with your father."

She shrugged. "What's there to tell? You saw how we are close up and personal."

"Has it always been strained?"

Sadie thought over her childhood. There was a time when things had been different. She halted in the middle of the path. "No. Everything changed when Bobby died." Why hadn't she seen that before?

"Who's Bobby?"

"My baby brother. He was three and I was nine. He died of a massive infection that had started out as a spider bite."

He came to her, grasping both her hands. His scent chased away all others. "I'm sorry we have that in common. Losing a sibling is so hard."

"But until this moment I never thought about Dad changing. He was always demanding, but loving and caring, usually. After Bobby's death he got worse, never satisfied with anything I did. It was never good enough for him. I always felt I had let him down, that I wasn't the son he had wanted."

"Maybe he's scared."

"Dad?"

"Yes. When you lose someone close to you, sometimes you shut down, afraid to feel anything for anyone."

"Is that experience talking?"

He ignored her question and began walking again, his pace faster. She started to pursue the question, but the firm set to his jaw proclaimed the subject was off-limits. She clamped her mouth shut. She didn't need him to say yes. She had seen the truth in his eyes before he masked his expression. His feelings shut down the day he lost his family, and Tom's death only cemented Andrew's determination not to care for another. When he was young, all the people he loved had died. How could she combat that?

Chapter Nine

"Everyone, I want you to meet Andrew, my knight in shining armor," Sadie announced to the group of friends sitting in her living room.

"Okay, you have managed to embarrass me," Andrew whispered in her ear.

"But it is true," she said with a laugh, trying to ignore his breath tickling her neck. "You've saved my work program. I've already recruited another business because IFI is participating."

"I know it hasn't been quite two weeks, but Chris seems to be doing a good job. He's got his route down for the mail run. He always has a smile for everyone. When he comes into my office, he usually stops to say hello if I'm not busy with someone."

"Good. He does brighten a person's day." She swept her arm in a wide arc. "Mingle. I'll let everyone tell you their names. I still have a few more things to put on trays so I can bring them in."

"Need any help?"

"Oh, no. I'm not gonna let you hide out in the kitchen."

"Madam, I never hide out. I was trying to fulfill the role of knight in shining armor and help." The corners of his mouth twitched.

"Sure, Andrew. These are just a few of my friends from school." She gently shoved him toward the group of eight people who were seated in the living room.

"You are cruel, Sadie Spencer."

The laughter in his voice contradicted his words. She gave him a little wave, then headed for the kitchen. She quickly finished preparing the trays and took the first one into the living room, halfway expecting to see Andrew off to the side by himself. Instead, she found him in the middle of the group, laughing at something Sally said. Then Carol made a comment that set everyone off.

"I hope you all have worked up an appetite. I have lots of food to get rid of." Sadie placed the tray on the coffee table and started for the kitchen.

"I'm not sure it's a good thing when a cook announces she must get rid of food," Andrew said, relaxing in the easy chair.

At the door into the kitchen, Sadie said, "Dig in at your own peril. Be back in a sec with more goodies." She heard people moving, and someone sighing with pleasure as he tasted one of her chocolate chip cookies.

She picked up another tray and headed for the door. It swung open. Andrew entered, finishing a brownie.

"I thought the least I could do was help you carry the trays to the living room. This brownie is to die for."

Sadie beamed. "Thanks—I think."

With Andrew's assistance the food was set up on the coffee and end tables so everyone could munch while talking. When Andrew tried to have Sadie sit in the easy chair he'd occupied, she shook her head and sat cross-legged on the floor in front of it.

"Okay, what game do you have for us this time?" Carol asked, taking a sticky bun from a plate.

"Truth or dare?" Sadie waved away the platter of assorted cookies making its rounds.

Sally and Ted groaned.

"How about Trivial Pursuit?" Nathan suggested.

"I'm brain dead. Besides, I got creamed the last time we played." Carol tore off a piece of the sticky bun and popped it into her mouth.

Ted laughed. "You always say that."

"I refuse to remember trivial facts. They clutter up my mind." Carol pointed a finger at Ted. "And not a word from you about that last comment."

Sadie held up her hand. "I guess as usual I'll have to settle this lively debate. We're gonna play charades. We haven't played that in a long time. The guys against the gals."

"Yes! We're gonna cream you," Joyce said to Ted.

Andrew leaned down and whispered into Sadie's ear, "We could just talk."

She shook her head. "You saw the debate about what game to play. You ought to see some of our discussions. Not a pretty sight. This is much safer."

"Did I hear the word safe?" Sally's husband, Mason, reached for another piece of fudge. "Sadie, if you think playing charades will be safe, you've got another think coming. Remember the reason we haven't played it in a long time. The gals cheat."

"We do not!" All of them spoke at the same time.

"We haven't played because you guys are sore losers." Sadie rose and went to a cabinet to retrieve the bag of choices. "And since we won last time, we get to pick which category." She produced a red cloth bag. "Movies it is."

When she sat down next to Andrew, he moved forward on the edge of his chair. "What if we haven't seen a movie in years, have no idea what is current?"

"No problem. Most of these are oldies. Late night TV fare."

"Worse. I don't watch TV unless it has something to do with the food industry. I don't even own one."

Sadie's attention was riveted to him. "You're kidding. You don't watch any shows."

"Nope. Don't have the time to watch."

"You do work a lot." He really did have this work thing bad, Sadie realized. She patted his arm. "Well, do the best you can."

"I think you're gloating, Sadie Spencer. I have to

tell you I am a fierce competitor. That should make up for my lack of knowledge.''

The glitter in his eyes could only be described as predatory. She shivered. ''So am I.''

''Then may the best man win.''

''You mean woman.''

Andrew winked. ''We'll see.''

An hour later half the food was gone and the score for charades was tied. Sadie and Andrew were the last ones. They were seated across the room from each other. Sadie eyed Andrew in the middle of the group of men and decided she'd created a monster. He'd immersed himself in the game with relish, and even though he hadn't watched many movies, he had come up with a surprising number of right answers.

Sadie shoved her hand into the red bag and drew her selection. She read it and wanted to moan. *Zulu.* Mason flipped the egg timer over, giving her one minute to think of what she would do. What in the world was *Zulu?* A war movie? How was she going to act this one out?

''Time's up,'' Andrew announced with more glee than he should.

Since everyone knew it was a movie, she held up one finger to indicate one word, then she motioned how many syllables and that she was giving them the first one. Hunching over, she made her arms swing back and forth like a trunk on an elephant—at least that was what she hoped it looked like.

''*Hunchback of Notre Dame,*'' Sally shouted.

"Yeah, that's one word with two syllables," Mason said.

"No comments from the peanut gallery." Carol moved closer to Sadie, as though that would enlighten her.

Sadie decided to portray another animal. She got down on all fours and acted like she was roaring—silently, of course, because the men would have declared foul for saying something. Surely she looked regal as she pranced as though she were the king of the jungle.

Joyce jumped up. "Cat."

Sadie lumbered to her feet to encourage Joyce to expand her answer.

"Tiger. Jaguar. Lion."

Sadie spread her arms wide as though to take in everything.

"*Lion King,*" Carol said.

Ted chuckled. "Two syllables, not two words."

Another animal. Sadie began leaping around the area, pounding on her chest and scratching her sides.

"Ape," Sally yelled.

Sadie nodded.

"Ape-man?"

"Is that supposed to be a movie?" Nathan asked, a smug expression on his face. "I thought you might say *Planet of the Apes.*"

Joyce flashed her husband a too sweet smile. "Can't. That's more than one word. Can't you count?"

Mason whistled. "I think she got you there, Nathan."

Before the whole thing fell apart, Sadie quickly went to the second syllable, noticing that over half her time was gone. She pantomimed washing her hands.

"Clean. Dirty."

"Eat."

Sadie continued with putting on makeup.

"Face."

"Beauty."

She tried brushing her hair.

"Bathroom."

Sadie waved her hand to get Sally to say more.

"Rest room? Women? Men?"

The timer went off. Sadie's shoulder slumped and she plopped down on the couch. *"Zulu."*

"Zulu?" Carol wrinkled her brow. "I guess the first was animals for zoo, but what was the last part?"

"Loo is the British word for restroom."

Sally rolled her eyes.

"I was desperate," Sadie said in her defense.

Andrew stood and dug into the bag for his selection. "If we win this, we win it all." He looked at his slip of paper and smiled, then handed it to Sadie.

Battle of the Bulge. Okay, the gals might still have a chance—if the sun rose in the west. She passed the paper down the row of women, hearing the groans as it made its way to the end.

After disclosing how many words in the title,

Andrew launched in with the first one. He punched the air.

"Fight." Mason waved his hand. "I know. *Fight at Okay Corral.*"

"At least my husband can count."

"No, he can't. The title is *Gunfight at the O.K. Corral.* That certainly is more than four words." Joyce crossed her legs and brushed imaginary lint from her jeans.

Andrew began firing a pretend machine gun.

"The Guns of Navaronne," Ted shouted.

Andrew held up one finger.

"Oh, sorry."

Next Andrew acted like he was fighting with a sword.

"Duel."

"War and Peace. War of the Roses."

Andrew shook his head.

"Battle."

Andrew nodded vigorously, pointing to Ted. Then Andrew indicated the fourth word. He puffed out his cheeks and held out his arms as though he weighed four hundred pounds.

Mason leaped up. "Fat. Obese. *Battle of the Bulge.*"

"Yes!" Andrew pumped his arm in the air.

She should have been upset that the women lost, but Sadie couldn't take her eyes off the huge grin on Andrew's face or forget the fact that he was high-fiving all the men as they congratulated themselves for their victory.

When the group settled down, Sadie found herself next to Andrew on the couch. Her side was pressed against his while four of them crammed themselves on the large sofa. Andrew shifted and placed his arm along the back cushion, which caused Sadie to be cradled in the crook of his arm. It felt right, she decided.

"I thought you said you didn't watch movies," Sadie said, content within the shelter of his arm.

Andrew smiled, a warm gleam in his eyes. "I don't, but I do love a good puzzle. In fact, I'm quite good at solving puzzles."

"Well, I dare say the guys will be wanting you to come back the next time."

"But not you?" Mischief brightened his eyes.

"I didn't say that."

"I could always restrain myself."

"You? Never. That's not in your nature."

His gaze pinned her. "What is in my nature?"

Suddenly Sadie felt as though they were the only two people in the room. Everything faded from her consciousness but Andrew and the intensity of his look. "You like to control the situation, be in charge. You thrive on challenges." She tilted her head to the side. "You're a loner, but I'm not sure that's what you truly want to be."

One brow arched. "And how did you come to that conclusion?"

She shrugged. "Woman's intuition?"

"When a woman doesn't want to answer a question, she falls back on that."

"What does a man fall back on?"

"Silence."

"You're quite good at that."

"It has come in handy from time to time."

Sadie chuckled. "I bet."

"Care to share what's so amusing?" Sally asked while sharing the easy chair with her husband.

Sadie slanted a glance toward Andrew. "We were discussing the differences between a man and a woman."

"Hold everything. I want this evening to end on a friendly note. I'm afraid if we go down that path my wife's radical views will start a war." Mason squeezed his wife to him, affection in his expression.

"We could always have Andrew act out the word *war*. He was getting quite good at the end." Sally leaned forward and grabbed another brownie.

For the next hour the discussion ranged from how different men and women were to the weather, which Sadie insisted was a safer topic of conversation. Slowly the evening wound down and her guests started to leave. When she closed her front door on Sally and Mason, she turned into the living room to find Andrew was the only one left. He transferred the few cookies on one tray to another, then stacked them to carry into the kitchen.

"You don't have to help clean up."

He glanced toward her. "I know. I want to."

Sadie tried to cover her surprised expression, but she realized she didn't.

"With both of us cleaning up, it won't take long." Andrew headed for the kitchen with the trays.

Sadie remained in the middle of the living room, still trying to shake off the shock. Her father never helped her mother clean up a thing. Even Thanksgiving Day she and Andrew had returned to the house to discover her mother doing all the work with her father watching.

When Sadie finally roused herself to follow Andrew into the kitchen, she found him searching under the sink for some dishwashing soap.

"What are you gonna do with the leftovers?"

"Give them to you?"

His laughter saturated the air like a warm coat in the dead of winter. "I think you spend half your time trying to fatten me up. I'll take a care package, but I'm only one man. There's no way I can finish all this off." He motioned toward the two trays still half filled with goodies.

"Thankfully I have a class who loves sweets. I'll take the rest to school and let them indulge on Monday."

"They must love you."

She blushed under his ardent perusal. "They do like it when I clean out my freezer."

"Come over here and dry." Andrew dunked the first tray into the soapy water.

"First, let me fix up your care package and put the rest into plastic bags."

They worked side by side in silence for a few minutes. Again the feeling of rightness descended over Sadie. When she picked up a towel to dry the large trays, she watched Andrew wipe down her counter and thought how much he looked at home in her kitchen. That realization brought her up short. She sucked in a deep breath and held it until her lungs burned.

While she put away the trays, Andrew prowled the room, coming to a stop at her desk. He stared at the pad, then lifted it and studied it.

"Is this scenery for a play?"

She nodded, bending to push the last tray to the back of the lower cabinet. "I'm in charge of the Christmas play at church this year. I'm trying to come up with the scenery needed. As you can see, I'm not a good artist."

For a few seconds a faraway look came into his eyes. "I used to be in stagecraft when I was in high school. I enjoy—" He bit off the rest of his sentence.

"You used to enjoy making scenery?" She straightened, facing Andrew.

"Yes. I used to like working with my hands. Something about it—" he paused, creasing his brow "—was comforting."

"Well, then, do I have a deal for you. I don't have anyone to build the scenery yet. I sure could use your help."

He shook his head. "I don't think—"

She walked to him and pressed her fingers across his mouth. "Please. Wouldn't it be nice to see if you still feel the same way?"

He sighed, his breath fanning her fingers.

She dropped her hand to her side and waited. Suddenly it was important that he became a part of the Christmas play.

"Okay, if I can find the time."

"Good. The first rehearsal is tomorrow afternoon. You can come and get an idea of what we're gonna do. Some of the high school youth group will be there. A few have volunteered to help with the pounding of nails. I just need a leader to direct them. And you have such good leadership qualities."

He laid his arms on her shoulders, trapping her in front of him. "And you have such good persuasive qualities. I think I'm doomed."

"We could always have real animals. That should be entertaining." Andrew stretched his long legs out in front of him and relaxed in the chair in the recreational hall at the church.

"Not to mention messy," Sadie said with a glance at him. "No, I think your idea of making animals would be better. With a cast of thirty first, second and third graders, I think that's about all I can handle in any one day."

"Okay, I can get some plywood and make animal cutouts, then have the high schoolers paint them. Didn't you say Cal was a budding artist?"

She nodded.

"Think he could do a cow, sheep and donkey?" Andrew drew in his legs as a small child ran in front of him and leaped over them.

"Jared, no running," Sadie called to the first grader. "Yes, Cal can handle that."

"While he's doing that, Chris and I can build the manger."

"Then you'll make the scenery?" Sadie sat next to Andrew.

"Yes, and I'll definitely have the easier of the two jobs." Andrew surveyed the large room filled with the thirty children waiting for Sadie to direct them. "Where's your help?"

"Carol should be here soon."

"It will just be you and Carol?"

"And now you," she said with a grin as she pushed to her feet and started for the group of children.

"I didn't say anything about working with the kids," Andrew called.

Sadie kept walking as if she didn't hear him when Andrew knew she'd heard every word he had uttered. He watched her gather the older children to her and begin giving instructions, her voice firm but caring.

A natural teacher. She'd make a good mother to his— He put an immediate halt to that thought, shoving the longing to the back recesses of his mind. He had no business visualizing any kind of relationship with Sadie beyond friendship. When the New Year came, he would be drowning in work. Right now, before the holidays, he had a reprieve—a very brief one.

For the next hour Andrew worked with the four high school students, who included Cal and Chris, making plans for the scenery. When Sadie announced play practice was over, the room erupted with children talking and laughing. They had been relatively quiet during the practice, which still amazed Andrew.

"I'll get the wood, paint and supplies. We can start putting everything together next Saturday afternoon at two." Andrew closed his pad, where he had written down the materials he needed.

"Mr. Knight, I'll help you get them."

Andrew started to say he could take care of it himself, but one look at Chris's eager expression and he replied, "Sure. I'll pick you up at noon next Saturday."

"Great!" Chris leaped to his feet. "I'll be a big help."

As he hurried toward his mother, who stood in the doorway into the recreational hall, Sadie approached. "The least I can do is help, too."

"Now you offer to help with the scenery." Andrew looked skyward.

"I've been told I have great timing."

Andrew threw back his head and laughed while thirty young children ran, walked and skipped out of the hall.

"Besides, I have the money to purchase the materials."

"No, I'll take care of it. Consider it my donation." Andrew raked his hand through his hair and scanned the empty hall, silence prevailing for the moment.

He took a deep breath and caught a whiff of Sadie's perfume. He thought of Ruth's rose garden, and memories of the time they'd spent in New Orleans inundated him. The warning signs had been there. He'd never taken another person to his old homestead. Sadie had a way of working her way into his life without him even knowing it until it was too—

Whoa! He put a stop to that thought, too. He was in control. His emotions concerning Sadie were nothing more than friendship.

"Up for a cup of coffee? I don't want to go home yet." Sadie threaded her arm through his.

"Why?"

"My dad is over at my house talking with Mom. I figure I'll give them some space."

He covered her hand on his arm. "Are you avoiding your father?"

Her fingers tightened. "Yes. I don't want to complicate the situation. They're working on their problems. My presence might make things more uncomfortable."

He would have given anything to have a family. He still missed his parents and sister after all these years. He usually didn't allow himself to think about the past, but Sadie and her situation with her parents had forced the memories to surface.

"Have you ever talked with your father about how you feel?"

She halted her progress toward the door. "No, I wouldn't know where to begin. And don't tell me at the beginning. You saw how Thanksgiving dinner was."

"I didn't say it would be easy, but ignoring your

feelings or keeping them bottled up inside of you can't be good."

"This from the man who has such a firm control over his own emotions."

"But I don't have a father I need to come to terms with."

Her gaze locked with his for a few seconds before it slid away. "I'm afraid."

"What could be worse than what you are going through now?"

"An out and out rejection." She hung her head, her shoulders slumping.

He lifted her chin and peered into her eyes. "That's a risk I think you should take. You told me your relationship with him changed after your little brother died. I know losing a loved one can change a person inside. Perhaps your father is suffering more than anyone knows."

She heard the anguish in his words. She doubted he realized it. Through a blur of tears, she laid her hand over his heart, feeling the slow beat beneath her fingertips. "And you've got no one to talk to about what happened to you all those years ago."

"There's nothing for me to talk about."

His heartbeat increased, negating his words. "Are you sure about that, Andrew? Maybe you should have a conversation with God. I think He's the one you're angry at."

He stepped back, his expression closed. "I'm not angry at anyone."

"You aren't? Then why don't you attend church? You used to. What happened?"

"Life. Work."

"That's a cop-out. If it's important, you make room for it in your life."

"I'm here now." He gestured wildly at the foyer leading into the sanctuary.

"That's not the same thing. When was the last time you spoke with the Lord?"

He took a bracing breath, visibly fighting for the control that was so important to him. "It's not going to work, Sadie. You're good at changing the subject when you don't want to discuss something."

"And you aren't?"

One corner of his mouth lifted. "Yes, we both are."

She grasped his hands in hers and held them up. "I'll make a deal with you. I'll speak with my father if you'll come to church with me and speak with God."

He closed his eyes for a moment, his chest rising and falling rapidly. "I'll come to church with you, but I can't guarantee anything beyond that."

"It's a start."

"And how about your part of the bargain?"

"I'll talk to my father."

"When?"

"Soon. That's all I can promise."

"I can live with that."

"Now, how about that cup of coffee and maybe a slice of pie, too?"

"If I hang around you too much longer, I'll have to start watching my weight. I still have several goodies from last night."

"You'll just have to start exercising more." Sadie linked her arm through his and started for the door, a lightness to her step. She liked the idea of him hanging with her—probably too much, if she wanted to avoid heartache. The problem with that was her heart was already involved, and she didn't think that was going to change any time soon.

Chapter Ten

"You can stop laughing now." In the church's recreational hall, Sadie took another step back from the cow she'd put the finishing touches on.

Andrew pressed his lips together, but his eyes held merriment deep within them.

"But, Miss Spencer, you got paint all over you," Chris exclaimed, not able to contain his laughter.

"Okay, so I got carried away. The cow is done. You and Cal are still painting the donkey." Sadie pointed her brush at the plywood animal in question.

"That's because this is gonna be a work of art. Right, Chris?" Cal dipped his brush into the bucket.

"Yeah, a work of art."

"And what is this?"

Andrew burst out laughing. "I think if we turn it around we can paint the other side and no one will be the wiser. When are the children going to be here?"

"In a few minutes. You aren't trying to get rid of me, are you?"

"Never." The gleam of merriment in Andrew's eyes brightened.

Sadie narrowed her gaze and directed its full force on the exasperating man. "My cow isn't that bad."

"I've never seen a brown and white one quite like that. The markings look like big polka dots."

"It's a Holstein."

"They're black and white, and their dots aren't that round. Besides, I doubt a Holstein was in the manger the evening Christ was born."

"Well, that will be the last time I offer you a little help while I'm waiting for the children to arrive."

"Promise? I think I hear the children in the foyer. You'd better check."

Glancing toward the door, Sadie cocked her head to the side. "I don't hear anyone."

When she looked at Andrew, he'd turned the plywood around to show the unfinished side, and all three of them had moved to stand in front as though that would block her view. She fisted her hands on her waist, screwed her mouth into a mock frown and tapped her foot against the tiled floor. "Do I have to remind you guys that I'm the director? Therefore I am in charge."

Andrew stalked toward her, his brush still in his hand. She eyed it, then looked into his face, set with determination. She took a big step backward and came up against a chair. When he stopped in front of her, she licked her dry lips and thought about making a mad dash for the door.

"If you stay, I can't be accountable for my actions. I have this overwhelming need to paint a polka dot—" with lightning speed he lifted his hand and brushed black paint on her cheek "—here, to match your cow, of course."

"Oh, you didn't!" She brought her hand up to her face and felt the wet paint.

"He did, Miss Spencer," Chris called, laughter in his voice. "Way to go, Mr. Knight."

"Chris, don't forget who your teacher is." Sadie started around Andrew, stumbled into him, grasping his hand with the brush before he realized it and snatching it away. As quickly as she secured the brush, she wiped it across his face from forehead to chin then scrambled away.

Andrew spun. Chris and Cal's laughter echoed through the recreational hall.

"You look like a zebra," Chris said.

"No, Chris. He doesn't have enough stripes—yet." Sadie went to the bucket and immersed the bristles in the black paint. "But I wouldn't want to be accused of not being authentic in my work." She held the brush up and strode toward him.

Andrew's eyes glittered. That should have been a warning to Sadie that she was in big trouble, but she was too elated at getting his brush that she ignored his stance, which spoke of a man ready to do battle.

Before she had a chance to raise her arm, he pinned

it flat against her side. She couldn't move. "I think I do hear the children."

"Too late. Where do you want it?"

"What?"

"The stripe."

"I—" She swallowed her words.

"Don't care, do you?"

"Andrew, the children!"

His gaze trekked downward. "Have you taken a good look at yourself? I don't think it will matter what I do."

Sadie glanced at her old, faded jeans and gray sweatshirt. For the first time she noticed how much brown paint she'd managed *not* to get on the piece of plywood.

"Oh!" Her gaze slipped to Andrew's face. "I was never a neat painter in school. My teachers were always complaining."

"I can see why."

The door to the hall burst open, and several children raced into the room. Sadie turned a pleading look on Andrew.

He leaned close until she felt surrounded by his scent. "This isn't over, Sadie. Just postponed."

"What are you going to do?" She moved an arm's length away.

"I have to think on that one. In the meanwhile, I need to scrub this stripe off." He casually walked past the people filing into the hall as though he wore a black line down his face every day.

But Sadie did see him tense when snickers erupted

from the children he passed. *Oh, my, I'm going to have to stay out of his way.* She wondered how long it would take for him to forget about the stripe.

Then she saw several little girls pointing to her face and giggling behind their hands. That was when Sadie remembered the big polka dot Andrew had painted on her cheek. She hurried after him, saying to the gathering group, "I'll be right back. Sit in the chairs and wait on me."

Ten minutes later, with her face scrubbed, she entered the recreational hall to find the children running around the room and Andrew trying to calm them down and get them into their chairs. The dismay reflected in his expression told her more than anything that this man wasn't used to being around six-, seven- and eight-year-olds. She stood by the door for a few minutes to give him a chance to subdue the masses.

After one seven-year-old boy knocked over a chair, Sadie took pity on Andrew and hurried forward, stopping next to him. Over the din he said, "Don't ever leave me alone with them again."

"I didn't leave you alone. Surely a few children aren't fright—"

"Don't say it. I will readily admit I'm scared of anyone under the age of fifteen and I'm definitely out of my element."

"With some practice you'd get the hang of it. You're a smart man."

"A smart man would have taken one look at the chaos and run the other way."

Sadie laughed, put her two fingers into her mouth

and blew a loud whistle that immediately got the children's attention. They stopped where they were and faced her, the noise level down to a low murmur.

"That's much better. Now I would like the shepherds to sit over here, the wise men here." Sadie pointed where she wanted them. "Angels in this row and Mary, Joseph and the innkeeper in front."

All the children dutifully made their way to their designated area.

"I'm amazed. They listened. Where did you learn to whistle like that?"

"My first year coaching. It's a great way to get children's attention. It's one of many survival techniques that I learned early on."

"Since you have everybody under control, I'll just return to the scenery and correct a few things."

Andrew left Sadie standing in front of the children and hurried to the half assembled scenery. After fixing Sadie's cow, he peered up to see her working with the angels. With a smile on her face and a calm demeanor, she looked like an angel herself.

He watched her give them their instructions and marveled at how they listened to her when only fifteen minutes before they were wild. He had thought they had been incapable of settling down. Another thing he was wrong about. With Sadie he was discovering that a lot.

He started to return his attention to the crib he was constructing when he saw a little boy with tears streaming down his face run to Sadie. She knelt so she was on the child's level and comforted him as he told her how he had bit his lip and it was bleeding. She withdrew a tissue from her pocket and dabbed at his mouth, her words low but soothing. The child calmed down and hastened back to his group.

Sadie Spencer would make a great mother and should have children of her own to love and care for. That thought popped into Andrew's mind, and he couldn't shake it, or the disconcerting feeling that washed through him. Picturing her with another man didn't sit well with him, either. That realization sent his mild discomfort into a full-fledged panic.

He had no claim on Sadie, and yet he couldn't shake the feeling he wanted to. There was no room in his life for a wife, and he couldn't see Sadie as anything but that. Yes, right now he had more time than he usually did, but that was only because it was the holidays, and work at IFI slowed down. Once the new year came he would be so busy he would lose track of whether it was night or day.

Nope, he had no business even thinking of Sadie in any terms except as a friend. She might be mother material, but he wasn't father material.

"Chris, I'll tell you when to pull the curtains open." Sadie paused by the young man and peeked into the audience to see if everyone was seated. Her parents and Andrew were in the front row. Her mother slipped her arm through her father's and leaned over to whisper something into his ear. Her father smiled.

Her mother had returned to her own home a few days ago on the condition that they continue in therapy. Much to Sadie's surprise her father had agreed, even coming to her house to help her mother pack and move home. Sadie hoped everything worked out for her parents, but she didn't know if that was possible. Her father wasn't having an affair; he was just consumed with his work. He'd never seemed in the past to be willing to make any changes. It had always been her mother bending to his will.

"Miss Spencer?"

A shepherd tapped her on the arm to get her attention. Sadie blinked and looked down. "Yes, Joey."

He crossed his legs and screwed his face into a frown. "I've got to go to the bathroom *bad.*"

Sadie glanced at her watch and noted it was time to begin. "Hurry. I'll wait for you to come back before we start."

"I'll be fast."

She surveyed the stage to make sure everything was in place, including the cast. One angel scratched her head, and her halo fell to the side. Joseph pulled on his fake beard, and it caught on his chin. Sadie quickly corrected the problems, then stepped to scan the area again.

She encountered a solid wall of flesh.

Andrew steadied her. "I was sent back here to check and make sure everything was okay."

"Who sent you?"

"Your mother. She remembers when she was the

director of the pageant and figured you might need some help.''

"I've got everything under control.''

The second she said that, Joey raced back, yelling so loud everyone in the audience must have heard, "I'm done going to the bathroom, Miss Spencer.''

Sadie winced.

Joey slid to a stop but not before colliding with a cow. It crashed to the floor, dust flying everywhere. One of the angels jumped back and fell against a donkey, which toppled, causing a chain reaction. Sadie squeezed her eyes closed and listened to the falling scenery, flinching every time she heard another piece hit the floor.

Then there was total silence, not even a sound from the audience on the other side of the curtain.

Afraid to look, Sadie pried one eye open.

All the children stood amidst the fallen scenery with their eyes round as saucers and their mouths agape.

"I'm sorry, Miss Spencer,'' Joey cried, tears coursing down his cheeks.

Practicing her deep breathing, she hurried to Joey and knelt in front of him. "That's okay. I know you didn't mean to do this.'' She tried not to look at the chaos around her, but her gaze—as though it had a will of its own—skimmed over the mess. "We'll put it right, and the play will go on.''

"Okay, kids. Pick up any pieces near you and stand them up.'' Andrew strode among the children and helped where needed.

Sadie watched as the stage was once again transformed into a stable. She marveled at how efficient Andrew was in getting the cast to assist him. While Andrew was dealing with the cleanup, Sadie parted the curtains and quickly stepped out in front, raising her hands to signal for the audience to quiet down.

"There has been a slight delay. If everyone will remain in their seats, we should be starting very soon."

"That sounded more like an earthquake struck," a man in the back called.

"We had a minor mishap with no injuries."

"Do you need any help?" her mother asked, her brow creased in worry.

"No, I have everything under control." She crossed her fingers behind her back and hoped she was right.

When she looked backstage, the scenery and the children were standing in their proper place. "Okay, it's time to begin." She moved off the stage with Andrew and signaled to Chris to open the curtains.

As they parted, Sadie whispered to Andrew, "I thought you didn't know anything about children."

"I don't, but I do know how to deal with a crisis."

"You have the makings of a father," she said without thinking, and immediately regretted the statement.

Andrew tensed, his expression shuttered. "You have to be around to be a father."

Reverend Littleton cut the birthday cake for Baby Jesus, then handed the plate to the first child in line.

Sadie poured the little girl a cup of punch. When she gave her the drink, Sadie's gaze found Andrew in the crowd. The intensity in his eyes took her breath away. She nearly spilled the next cup. Determinedly she kept her attention on her task, but the hair on the nape of her neck tingled. If she glanced up, she would find Andrew looking at her. That thought disconcerted her but at the same time sent a thrill through her.

"The play was lovely, dear," an older lady said as she stood behind her grandson in line for refreshments. "Of course, when I did it, Joseph didn't forget his lines, and we used a live sheep."

"Yes, Henrietta, I remember that sheep well. Didn't it eat the hay in the manger, then baa the whole way through the play?" Robert Spencer asked, coming up behind Sadie.

The older woman turned beet red and hustled her grandson away with his drink and cake.

"You remember that?"

"Yes. That was the year you were Mary."

"I didn't know you came. I thought you couldn't make it."

"I was in the back and had to leave right after the performance, but I was there to see you woo the audience."

Sadie flushed, never expecting to hear those words from her father. She slanted a look at him and wondered what had happened to him. He didn't compliment. She continued to fill cups with punch, deciding she had better not say anything about this out-of-character action. Instead, she basked in the praise.

"Can I get two glasses for me and your mom?"

"Yes," she said, quickly pouring for her father.

"We're going to leave, but we'll see you tomorrow. Invite your young man if you want, Sadie. I like him."

Her father left her staring at his retreating figure, stunned at what had just transpired.

"Miss Spencer, I'm thirsty," Joey said, thrusting a cup toward her.

"Oh, sorry." She quickly refilled his glass, then finished serving the rest of the lineup.

When she was through, she poured herself and Andrew a cup and headed toward him. Reverend Littleton paused beside Andrew, said a few words, then moved on toward a group of men near Andrew. He watched the reverend progress through the crowd, a thoughtful expression on his face.

As Sadie neared Andrew, their gazes locked, and she felt as though the rest of the people vanished, leaving only her and Andrew in the hall. She remembered her father's words. *Your young man.* Suddenly she realized she wished that were true. She liked Andrew, too, much more than she should. She was afraid she was even falling in love with him.

"What did the reverend want?"

"That he hoped to see me at church."

"I hope you're thirsty." She handed Andrew his cup, not sure what to say. The fact she was falling in love wiped everything from her mind but the man before her.

"I saw your parents sneaking out of here."

Sadie glanced toward the double doors and visualized her and Andrew doing the same. She wanted to be alone with him to explore this new revelation. "Mom says Dad is trying to be more responsive to her needs. She thinks her leaving him really shook him up."

"I'm glad it's working out for them."

"So am I. I hated the idea of them divorcing."

"That seems to be the trend."

"Not in my book. My word means a lot to me. If I pledged myself to another, I would want it to be for life." She thought about her growing feelings for Andrew and panic took hold. If she fell totally and completely in love with him, she could never see herself in a relationship with another man—even if Andrew didn't return her love. She needed to back away from him before it was too late.

"Your pageant was a success."

"I couldn't have done it without your help."

"Yes, you could have. You're a very capable woman."

She warmed under his compliment. She was capable and independent, but she realized she'd enjoyed working on the pageant these past few weekends with Andrew, sharing duties, brainstorming the best way to do something. It was nice not being alone for once.

"I'm glad it's over with. I intend to relax for the rest of my Christmas vacation. The end of the semester at school and all the holiday preparations have exhausted me. Ready to leave?"

"Yes. I like the idea of relaxing." Andrew tossed

down the rest of the punch, then took her cup and threw both cups away.

As they made their way toward the door, Sadie asked, "Is my hearing correct? You said you like the idea of relaxing?"

He placed his hand at the small of her back and guided her from the recreational hall. "Yes, you heard me. You must be rubbing off on me."

"Don't say that too loud. Someone might think you went off the deep end."

"If I do, you're going with me." Clasping her hand, he stepped into the night.

Large snowflakes swirled on the light breeze, dancing in the lights in the parking lot. "We might have a white Christmas! It's been years since we have." She breathed in the crisp, cold air laced with the scent of burning wood.

"This might spoil some people's plans."

"I don't think it will snow much, and I doubt the children will much care. They'll be having too much fun, sledding and building snowmen."

"Is that what you did as a little girl?"

"Sure. Didn't—"

Andrew shook his head. "Remember, I grew up in New Orleans. I don't remember seeing snow until I moved here."

"I like snow as a change of pace in the winter, but I wouldn't want to live too much farther north. I want my snow to fall, then melt in a few days." Sadie emerged from the overhang and turned her face toward the heavens, relishing the feel of snowflakes melting on her cheeks.

Andrew came up behind her and grasped her shoulders. "I still haven't grown accustomed to the cold weather. Let's get in the car before I freeze."

"It would have helped if you had worn a coat." She peered at him, dressed in a nice pair of black slacks with a black turtleneck and a multicolored wool sweater.

"It wasn't snowing when I left my house."

"Don't you listen to the weather?"

"Nope. I usually don't have the time. Besides, I figure what's going to happen will happen. So many times the predictions weren't right that I gave up on believing them."

"True. But that's Oklahoma weather for you. It's hard to predict."

"Then why listen?"

She shrugged, starting toward his car. "Habit."

"Do you do a lot of things out of habit?"

"I wouldn't say a lot. I like to be spontaneous."

Andrew chuckled. "I can vouch for that."

"Since you don't have a spontaneous bone in your body—"

"Hey, I think I resent that. I can go with the flow with the best of them."

"Oh, please, Andrew. Only when it's going your way."

He opened the passenger door for Sadie. "I will admit I prefer being in control to going with the flow."

She waited until he rounded the front of the car and slid behind the wheel before speaking. "You probably have a five-year plan that you haven't wavered from since you came up with it."

"What's wrong with having goals?" He started the engine and slowly backed out of the parking space.

"Nothing. Goals are fine so long as you keep them in perspective. Life happens. Changes occur."

"I know that. I met you, and you were nowhere in my five-year plan."

A sudden silence fell between them, thick and heavy. Sadie didn't know what to say to that revelation, and from the frown on his face, she was sure Andrew hadn't meant to admit something like that to her.

"I'm not sure how to take that," she finally said.

"It's a compliment. I don't allow many things to affect my five-year plan."

"And I do?"

"You've made me question my path, my goals."

"What conclusions have you come to?"

"The jury is still out."

The temperature in the car soared, and it had nothing to do with the heater. Hope blossomed in Sadie's heart, and for a moment she allowed it to grow. But then her doubts began to surface. She didn't think she wanted to be responsible for anyone changing the direction of his life. That put too much of a burden on her.

"I enjoyed going with you to church tonight. Reverend Littleton has a gift for inspiring others.'' Andrew pulled into her driveway.

"I love the early Christmas Eve service. The children take such a big part in it."

"I like the idea of a birthday celebration afterward. Nice way of reminding the children and adults why we celebrate Christmas."

"It's still early. Do you want to come in for some coffee—the decaf kind?"

"Love to."

When Sadie entered her house, the scent of pine and cinnamon assailed her. Her live tree dominated the living room, and the aroma from baking cookies hung in the air. She plugged in the lights before heading for the kitchen to make the coffee. Andrew followed.

"Your home is so inviting."

"I love to decorate. I probably go overboard."

"You think?" Andrew scanned the kitchen, filled with Christmas items, from the towels hanging on the stove to the canisters on the counter to the Christmas cards on the refrigerator.

"Okay. I do go overboard. But in my defense, it's hard not to get wrapped up in the holidays with the students I teach. A lot of the ornaments on the tree are made by them. Every year when I put them up, I think about the students who made them. To me it's like a photo album of memories. Do you have a tree?"

"No. I'm not home much to enjoy it."

His words evoked a sadness in Sadie that she

couldn't shake. She wanted to put her arms around him and tell him this Christmas he wasn't alone. Instead she prepared the coffee, her hands trembling, her throat tight. Andrew had lost his sense of family and home. The day of the fire, his house was not the only thing destroyed.

Dear Lord, help me to guide him back to You. He needs You. He needs to believe in belonging again.

The aroma of brewing coffee spiced the air, lending a homey warmth to the room. Sadie faced Andrew, leaning against the counter. Her smile quivered at the corners of her mouth. "If I had known that, Andrew Knight, I would have brought a tree to your house and helped you put it up."

"A pine without any decoration would have looked strange in the middle of my living room."

"You don't have any?"

He shook his head.

Sadie knew then what she would give him for Christmas, in addition to the mystery she had bought him. "Then you can enjoy my tree tonight and my parents' tomorrow. They wanted you to come to dinner. I think my father will behave this time."

"Are you gonna be there?" His eyes crinkled in a smile.

"Yes, and I would love for you to join us."

"Then in that case, I will."

"Good." Sadie twisted to pour two cups of coffee, then handed one to Andrew. "Let's sit in the living room."

She opened the blinds over the French doors that

led to the patio so they could watch the snow fall. With all the lights out except those on the Christmas tree, the room was dim and cozy, a magical feel to the atmosphere. Sadie sat next to Andrew on the sofa and let the silence between them lengthen.

"Do you have trouble driving in the snow?" she finally asked as the white on the ground deepened.

"No. I may be from New Orleans, but I manage to get around okay. In fact, I'll pick you up tomorrow morning to go over to your parents."

"I appreciate that. I may be from here, but I don't do well driving in the snow. I got stuck once on a hill. My car slid all the way down and into a ditch. I had to abandon it and walk to a store to call my father to come rescue me." The memory blazed across her mind, reminding her of yet another incident where she hadn't quite lived up to what her father had thought she should be able to do. He hadn't been pleased that she had interrupted his writing time.

"That can happen to anyone."

"Yes, I suppose it could," she murmured, pushing the memory into the background. "But still you'd better not stay too long. I don't think I could rescue you."

"I think you could do anything you set your heart to."

Sadie placed her half empty mug on a coaster on the coffee table. "I appreciate the compliment, but I'm still not gonna get out in this weather to tow you out of a ditch."

"Chicken."

She looked him directly in the eye. "Yes, and proud of it."

His laughter wove its magic about her. In that moment she knew the possibility she was in love with him was a reality. She also realized her heart would probably be broken by this man.

He put his cup down, too. "I think I'd better go. I wouldn't want to be tempted—to call you if I needed to be pulled out of a ditch."

She rose at the same time he did. They stood a foot apart between the sofa and the coffee table with little maneuvering room. "I—" She swallowed several times. "Will you go with me to the teacher banquet in a few weeks?"

"The one where they announce the teacher of the year for your school district?"

She nodded, acutely aware of the man so close she could reach out and touch the lines of his face.

"I'd love to. And when you win I intend to embarrass you with my applause."

A blush heated her cheeks. "I might not win. There are some good teachers up for the honor."

He moved closer and clasped her upper arms, his fingers rubbing circles. "If you don't win, that's their loss."

She thought for a moment he was going to kiss her, but instead he squeezed by her and walked toward the front door. On the porch he stopped and glanced at her.

"Drive safely, and call me when you get home."

His eyes widened for a few seconds. "I don't think anyone has ever said that to me."

"Then there's a first time for everything."

She watched him get into his car and pull out of the driveway. She waved to him, then waited until he was at the end of her street before she went into her warm house. She leaned against the front door and closed her eyes, imagining him with the snow falling around him, his footprints to his car marring the pristine white landscape.

She wanted him in her life. Would he disappear like his footprints in the continuing snowfall? She felt her heart crack with the answer.

Chapter Eleven

"I should have realized you had an ulterior motive when you insisted I bring my heavy coat." In Sadie's parents' foyer, Andrew zipped up his jacket and fitted his gloves on his hands.

"Trust me. You'll enjoy this. When I was growing up, I couldn't wait for a snowfall. I got out of school, but I also got to play in the snow. Everyone should at least once in his life build a snowman." Sadie tugged open her parents' front door and stepped into the crisp, cold air.

"I suppose if this was summer you'd have me running around catching fireflies and putting them in a jar."

"Oh, no. I don't believe in that. But I do like to watch them on a summer's night." She paused on the porch and scanned the blanket of white, the snow muffling any sounds.

"So where are you going to build this snowman?"

She quirked a brow at Andrew. "Me?"

"You don't seriously expect me to roll balls of snow around on the ground, do you?"

"Yes."

"Oh, all right." He exaggerated a sigh. "Let's get this over with."

"You don't have to act like this will be torture." Sadie marched down the steps and trudged into the yard. "We'll put it here." She bent over, packing some snow into a ball, then she began to roll it along the ground.

Andrew watched her for a good minute, then followed her lead. "I hope no one from the office drives by."

"This is a dead-end street. I think you're safe."

Fifteen minutes later Sadie had the bottom part done. Sweat beaded her forehead, and she swiped her gloved hand across her brow. "I forgot how much work this was."

"I thought we were playing." Andrew lifted his large snowball and placed it on top of hers.

"We are. Sometimes playing can be hard work."

"Are we through?"

"We are if you want a headless snowman. Tell you what, go inside and ask my mom for a carrot and a box of raisins. I'll finish the last part."

"And have your mother think I'm crazy? No, you go inside and get those things. I'll make the last ball."

"Mother's used to strange requests from me."

"Now that doesn't surprise me." Andrew started on the last snowball.

Sadie hurried inside and found the food she wanted to make the face. On her way out she noticed her father stacking logs in the fireplace. She loved sitting in front of a warm fire after being outside in the cold. She couldn't wait to share the cozy moment with Andrew and give him his presents.

When she emerged from the house, she found Andrew positioning the last snowball. He stepped back to examine his efforts. Sadie stuffed the carrot and box of raisins in her pocket, then leaned over, scooped up a handful of snow and packed it into a ball. Straightening, she threw it at Andrew. The snow sputtered against his overcoat. She quickly made another and aimed for his chest. The ball hit him in the side of the head because he moved at the last moment—toward her.

"I didn't mean to hit you in the face."

He kept coming, his intentions to get even clearly written in his expression. "That's okay. And I'm not gonna mean to do what I'm gonna do."

"What's that?" She squeaked the words and took a huge step back.

With lightning speed he closed the space between them, barreling into her and sending her into a snow pile. "This."

His massive body covered hers for a few seconds before he rose and offered her his hand. She gathered some snow and hurled it at his chest. His eyes widened, then narrowed on her.

"I was trying to be a nice guy, but this is war. I still remember the paint incident at play rehearsal."

Quickly he made several balls, then launched them at her. One hit her in the back as she scrambled to her feet, the other on her leg as she ran toward the porch. He stalked her, bending down every few feet to form another snowball and toss it at her. She managed to dodge the third one, but the fourth ball got her in the chest.

"Uncle! Uncle!" She glanced over her shoulder to see if Andrew had stopped his pursuit.

He was still coming with a relentlessness that must pay off in the business world.

She almost made it to the front door when he halted her escape inside.

He leaned close and whispered, "Where are you going? We haven't finished what we started."

"That depends on what you're talking about."

"The snowman. What else is there?"

His breath tickled the skin below her earlobe. She trembled, even though sweat ran in rivulets down her face. "You're not going to throw any more snowballs?"

"I won't if you won't."

"A deal." She released her hold on the doorknob and turned toward him. He smashed a ball into her face.

"You lied."

"I didn't. I didn't throw a thing."

She wiped the cold snow from her while peering at his other hand to make sure he didn't have anything in it.

"We're even now." He backed away, holding his

arms out. "I'll be good unless you decide to take me on again."

"I've learned my lesson. You fight dirty."

"I fight to win. I learned that long ago, Sadie."

His words, spoken with a hard edge, embedded coldness like a sweeping blizzard deep inside her. She needed to remember that. He was after the presidency of IFI, and nothing and no one would stand in his way. Heartache chipped at her composure.

Sadie quickly finished the snowman, arranging the carrot for the nose, two pieces of bark for the eyes and the raisins for the mouth. After sticking two broken limbs for arms into the middle snowball, she stood back and inspected their creation. He leaned to the left, and the balls weren't proportional, but she didn't care. Andrew and she had made it together, and even with his grumbling, she suspected he hadn't minded. He could play when forced to.

A cold breeze sliced through her, reminding her that her backside was wet from lying in the snow. She shuddered and hugged herself. "I think I need to get inside and warm up."

"I probably should be going soon. I certainly enjoyed the dinner. I appreciate your parents including me."

"And this time my father behaved himself." Sadie started for the house.

"Have you talked to him yet?"

She halted, as stiff as if a cold wind had ripped through her and frozen her. "I haven't found the right time."

"Don't wait too long, Sadie." Andrew came up beside her and took her hand. "I've never told anyone this, but my dad and I had a fight the evening of the fire. I ran up to my bedroom after shouting at him that I hated him. I never got to tell him I loved him, that I didn't mean what I'd said that night. I would give anything to be able to take those words back. But I can't, and it's too late to ask him to forgive me."

She grasped his other hand. "He knew you loved him and he forgave you. Children say things they don't mean. Parents know that."

"It doesn't change the way I feel. There's an emptiness inside of me that I can't fill."

"Seek God's guidance. He'll help you fill that void."

"I don't know if that's possible. I've lived so long with this hollow feeling." He brought their clasped hands to his chest, covering his heart.

"You're always welcome to go with me to church. The children love you, and Reverend Littleton is a wonderful listener. Look what he was able to do with my parents."

"Maybe your dad was ready and just needed a push."

"And maybe you're ready. Faith is a great healer, Andrew."

He cupped her face. "I'll think about it if you'll think about talking with your father."

"That was our deal." Emotions swelled in her

parched throat. "Now, I have something for you, and I can't wait another minute to give it to you."

"You got me a present?" Surprise laced his voice.

"Yes, I like to give presents to my friends."

He slid his hand into his pocket and withdrew a small wrapped box. "So do I."

"You got me a present?" The same surprise was in her voice as she took the gift from him.

"I started to give it to you ahead of time, but then I remembered you saying something about unwrapping presents before you should then rewrapping them so no one knew you peeked early."

"So you took the temptation away from me. Now that's what I call a friend."

Inside Sadie shed her overcoat, gloves and hat, then opened the closet door to retrieve his gifts. She handed them to him. "Let's open them in the living room."

When Andrew stepped into the room, he froze, every line of his body tensing. His gaze was riveted to the fire raging in the hearth. Emotions flooded his face, usually so controlled.

He swung around and left. "I can't."

Sadie hurried after him and caught him in the foyer as he was shrugging into his coat. "I'm sorry about the fire. I wasn't thinking. I should have said something to Dad about it. We always burn a yule log on Christmas Day."

"And you should. It's part of your tradition."

"Please don't leave just yet."

He inhaled a deep breath and held it. "I don't usually look back, and these past few days I've done more reflection than…'' His voice faded into silence as he glanced away from her. "I can't stay, Sadie. I need to be alone.''

He wrenched open the front door and walked away, leaving her staring at his retreating figure. She wanted to run after him; he had thrown up a barrier between them, erected over the years to protect his heart. Tears blurred her vision as she swung the door closed and felt the emptiness of the foyer.

Then she remembered the gift he had given her, still clasped in her hand. She carefully unwrapped it and lifted the lid. Beautiful gold earrings with hearts dangling from hoops lay nestled in red tissue. A small card was in the lid.

Sadie read the words, and her tears ran down her face. *To a lady with a heart of gold.*

Andrew sought refuge in his house with not one Christmas decoration to adorn its sterile decor. He slowly turned in his living room and scanned his possessions. The oak furniture was utilitarian and simple. The tables were devoid of knickknacks. The room reminded him of any number of suites he'd stayed in while traveling for business. Nothing personal. Nothing to tie him to the place. That was always how he'd wanted it—until now. Until Sadie. Now he dreamed of more.

But he wasn't good at relationships. For years he'd kept his emotions so tightly bottled up inside him that he'd lost the ability to express his true feelings. Because of that he certainly couldn't see himself getting married. With Sadie that would be the only way.

His gaze fell to the two wrapped presents she'd given him. He didn't make a move toward them, afraid to open the gifts because they would be personal—not like those he received from acquaintances and business associates. The presents on his coffee table mocked him, demanding to be opened.

He reached for them, a slight tremor in his grasp. He picked up the flatter of the two and quickly tore the paper away to reveal a mystery book by a popular writer. He flipped open the book to find that Sadie had inscribed a message to him. *For the day you decide to take a vacation and relax.*

His chest felt tight, each breath he inhaled searing his lungs. The tight lid on his emotions popped off, and a few leaked out.

When he unwrapped the second present, he took his time, wanting to prolong the discovery of what lay beneath the green foil for as long as he could. He opened the box and nearly dropped it. Inside was a hand-painted Christmas ornament with his name on it and a message that said, "The first of many."

Many what? Christmases together? Ornaments from her? He pushed the box away. What lay inside demanded too much of him. Didn't she know he wasn't capable of giving himself?

Andrew unlocked his front door and stepped to the side to allow Sadie past him. He wanted to give her something of himself—his time. It was a small gesture to arrange a special dinner for her, but he suspected she would appreciate it. "You really don't have to do this," Sadie said, entering Andrew's house for the first time, a delicious aroma of baking food drifting from the kitchen.

"Yes, I do. You've cooked for me on numerous occasions. Now it's my turn."

"But you can't cook."

"But I know how to order." Andrew held up his forefinger. "This is very good at dialing."

"I like a resourceful man."

"I aim to please." He showed her into the living room, taking her coat and laying it over the back of a chair.

Sadie stopped and stared at the Christmas ornament she had made for Andrew. It hung from a stand on an end table. Except for a beautiful hand-painted lamp, her gift to him was the only thing on the table. In fact, as she surveyed the room, the only other items that indicated this was a person's home were a photograph of Ruth, Darrell and their little girl and some magazines, all business related, scattered on the coffee table. This glimpse into Andrew's private life made her sad.

"Thank you for the gifts." Andrew sat on the black leather couch and motioned for her to sit also. "But I have to admit your ornament looks kind of lonely sitting over there by itself."

"I was hoping you'd feel that way and add to your collection of one."

"Stranger things have happened."

"With a few touches of color, a couple of pillows, this room—" she began with a wave of her hand.

"Don't, Sadie." Andrew pressed his finger against her mouth to still her words. "I'm rarely here. I spend more time in my office than here."

"What I saw of your office, you could use some color there, too, and a few knickknacks to personalize the place."

"Why? They only collect dust." He relaxed on the sofa.

"I guess that's one way of looking at it. I prefer to think of the various items I have around my house as mementos of my past."

"But you forget I don't dwell in my past."

"Don't you?"

"What do you mean by that?"

"I think your past very much dictates how you live now. You say you don't look back, but what happened to you in the past is what has made you the man you are today."

A frown creased his forehead, and he pinched his mouth into an unyielding line. "I suppose you have a point."

"I have my moments." Sadie sat up straighter, twisting so she faced Andrew on the couch. "Listen, about Christmas Day. I'm so sorry about the fire. I wasn't thinking."

He held up his hand to stop her flow of words. "I know you didn't mean anything by it. You would think a grown man could be in the same room as a fire, and usually I can. But for some reason I felt as though the walls were closing in on me.''

''My parents missed saying goodbye to you.''

''Please give them my apologies.''

''I already have. They understand.''

For a moment an uncomfortable silence pulsated between them. She felt as though she could hear his heart beating, and its fast tempo matched hers.

''How long did the snowman last?'' Andrew shifted on the couch, sliding his arm along the back cushion behind Sadie.

''About twenty-four hours. It toppled over before it completely melted. I'm not sure naturally or from the two boys across the street. Either way, it bit the dust. All that was left was the carrot and two pieces of bark. I think the birds took the raisins.'' She realized she was chattering, but she was nervous, as though this evening something would change between them.

The sound of her stomach rumbling drew a raised brow from Andrew. ''I suppose you're ready to eat.''

She nodded, a sheepish smile on her face. ''I forgot to eat lunch today.''

''No! Not you? The woman who lectured me on what a proper breakfast was?''

''I spent all day taking down my Christmas decorations. It was a huge task.''

''I can imagine, after seeing your house. Was there any room you didn't have something in?''

She thought for a moment, her head tilted to the side. ''Nope, not that I can think of. As a teacher I collect a lot of things at this time of year. I have to find somewhere to display them."

Andrew pushed himself off the sofa and turned to help her up. "A few of the decorations did look homemade."

She placed her hand in his and rose. "Those are my favorites. Anyone can go out and buy something. It means a lot to me when one of my students makes me something for the classroom or my house."

"I noticed you collect angels."

"And snowmen. Those were in the back bedrooms. I'm thinking of doing one of those Christmas villages."

"I think you're a kid at heart."

"Teaching students keeps me young."

"That from an old lady of thirty."

"I'll say that when I'm fifty. It's hard to be around young people and not be caught up in their exhilaration, their youthfulness."

"That's your fountain of youth?"

"You know, I never thought of it that way, but you're right. But I also need food, so lead the way."

"I must say you do a good job of ordering a delicious dinner." Sadie folded her napkin and placed it beside her empty plate. "What's for dessert?"

"You ask that after eating a healthy portion of prime roast beef, potatoes au gratin, steamed carrots and a Caesar salad, not to mention two rolls?"

"Yep. I always save room for dessert."

"Where? Your big toe?"

"Didn't you notice I ate extra slow? That way I have more room for what I'm sure will be something chocolate."

"You're very sure of yourself."

"You've admitted a weakness for chocolate just like me."

He scraped his chair back and gathered their plates. "Coffee?"

"Yes, please. Can I help?"

"No, you're my guest. Sit back and relax. I'll be just a minute."

Sadie took in her surroundings. The mahogany dining room table shone with a high polish, reflecting the chandelier's many crystal pieces. There was no china cabinet, but there was a buffet table with a silk flower arrangement that matched the one in the center of the table. The room dripped elegance, but again she felt its impersonal touch.

Andrew shouldered the kitchen door open and entered with two plates of chocolate fudge cake. After putting them on the royal blue place mats, he went back for the coffee, poured them a cup and sat down.

"Now this is what I call a real dessert," Sadie exclaimed, leisurely sliding the first forkful into her mouth and savoring the luscious taste.

When she'd finished the last bite, Andrew smiled and asked, "Another piece?"

"I'll take a rain check on that. Better yet, you can send a slice home with me. One for the last day of the old year and the first day of the new year."

"You have everything figured out."

"Not by a long shot." She rose. "Let's get these dishes cleaned up so we can greet the new year in proper style."

"And what's that?"

"I brought hats and horns for both of us."

"I haven't worn a silly hat since a birthday party when I was eight."

"Oh, good. Then you know how much fun we'll have," Sadie said as she pushed her way through the swinging kitchen door. She took the plates to the sink, and when Andrew entered, added, "This is one of the cleanest kitchens I've ever seen."

"That's because it's rarely used. Even tonight all I had to do was heat up the dishes. Simplicity is my middle name."

"I'll rinse the dishes while you put them in the dishwasher. You do know how to do that, don't you?"

"I'm not that hopeless in the kitchen."

"No, the dinner was heated to perfection."

"See, there's hope for me." Andrew took the first plate she rinsed.

Twenty minutes later, the kitchen was spotless again. Sadie dried her hands on a paper towel and tossed it into the garbage can under the sink. "I didn't realize it was so late. We only have twenty minutes until midnight."

"We got a late start, and you ate slow."

"Hurry. I want to get our hats."

"I was hoping you forgot about them," Andrew grumbled as he followed her into the living room.

She produced a bright gold hat with a point and red glitter, she set it on her head, then gave him one that was silver with blue sparkles. Next she pulled out of her bag two horns and some confetti. "Now we're ready, with fifteen minutes to spare."

"Do we just stand here and wait or can we relax on the sofa?"

"When was the last New Year's Eve party you went to?"

"Last year. I'm not as hopeless as you think."

"Did it have something to do with IFI?"

He looked uncomfortable, a tiny frown furrowing his brow. "The president gave a party for all the executives."

"That doesn't count."

He stepped toward her. "Yes, it does. A party is a party."

"Okay, maybe half." She moved closer to him.

They stood in the middle of his living room, their gazes trained on the clock on the mantel. Silence ruled as the minutes ticked by.

"Five. Four. Three. Two. Happy New Year," Sadie said, blowing her horn and tossing confetti into the air.

As bits of paper drifted down, Andrew closed the space between them and drew her into his arms. He bent forward and kissed her, his embrace tightening.

Her emotions swirled as though they were confetti caught in a breeze. His arms around her felt so right. Andrew Knight in her life felt right.

When he touched his forehead to hers, she breathed

in the scent of him and knew there would never be another man for her. She framed his face and compelled him to look her in the eye. "I love you, Andrew. I can't pretend otherwise any longer."

Everything came to a standstill for a long moment. It seemed as though her heart stopped beating, her breath trapped in her lungs.

Then all of a sudden he moved away from her. He placed several feet between then, tearing the silver hat off his head. Something akin to fear shone in his eyes as he stared at her. Then he shuttered his look and turned away.

"I'd better drive you home now. I have work to do tomorrow. And yes, I know it's New Year's Day and a holiday, but the work still has to be done." Andrew took her hand and squeezed it, his expression softening for a few seconds. "Things will start to heat up now that the holidays are over. I've played long enough."

Sadie felt a door slam shut in her face. He was securing his emotions against her, and she wasn't sure there was anything she could do about it. The crack in her heart widened.

Chapter Twelve

"**I**'m glad you could come so quickly, Miss Spencer." Mrs. Lawson motioned for Sadie to have a seat in front of her desk in her office at IFI.

"You said something about Chris having some problems at work that you wanted to discuss with me. What's wrong? Chris seems happy working here."

"Perhaps too much. That's the problem. When he delivers mail, I've seen him hugging some people in the offices or high-fiving others."

"I know he can be a bit enthusiastic when he sees someone he knows. Has anyone complained?"

"No, but that's not proper in a place of business."

"Have you talked with Chris about this?"

"No, I thought I would discuss it with you first. I've never dealt with someone—" the woman searched for her next words "—like Chris."

Sadie shifted, her hands clenching the arms of the chair. "Do you want me to talk to Chris?"

"That might be best," Mrs. Lawson said with relief in her voice.

Sadie rose, silently counting slowly to ten. She started for the door but stopped and pivoted. "Mrs. Lawson, Chris is just like anyone else working for you. If he's doing something wrong, I've often found him eager to change. He likes to please people."

Sadie left the woman's office before she said something that would ruin Chris's chances of working at IFI after graduation. She walked straight to Chris's station, touched his arm and indicated he follow her outside.

In the hallway Sadie pulled Chris over to the side for privacy. "How's it going?"

"Great. The people are nice."

"I'm glad you like it here. Chris, Mrs. Lawson feels you're too friendly with people when you greet them. Remember what I've always said about shaking people's hands."

"But I like them. I thought you hug people when you care."

"Not at a place of business. Can you remember that? It's important when you greet someone to say hi and shake his hand. No hugging or high-fiving. High-fiving is fine for school but not here."

"Yes, Miss Spencer. I'll remember."

The smile he gave her reassured her that he would try his best. "Good. Now, you'd better get back to work. I'll talk with you tomorrow at school."

"See you." Chris waved before going back into the mail room.

Sadie glanced at the bank of elevators at the end of the hall and wondered if Andrew was in his office. She wanted to tell him what time the dinner on Saturday started. Being a spur-of-the-moment kind of person, she headed for the elevator and rode up to his floor.

When she saw Mrs. Fox manning her desk, Sadie inhaled a deep, fortifying breath and approached. ''Is Andrew busy?''

''Yes.'' Mrs. Fox looked up, her mouth pinching into a thin line.

Sadie suspected the woman wasn't too happy about how she had circumvented her to get to Andrew. ''May I see him?''

''Just a moment.'' Mrs. Fox buzzed Andrew and announced Sadie was in the reception area. ''Go on in, Miss Spencer.''

''Thank you.'' Sadie flashed the woman a huge smile and walked to Andrew's door.

When she entered, he was already halfway across his office. ''I won't keep you. I just wanted to tell you when the teacher's dinner is.''

''This Saturday, isn't it?''

''Yes. It's at seven at The Garden.''

''Then I'll pick you up at six-thirty. I should be through with my meeting by then.''

Through with his meeting? A rift of unease shivered through her.

His phone rang. Andrew held up his hand and said, ''Just a moment.''

Striding quickly to his desk, he snatched up the

receiver and spoke low into it. Whatever the person on the other end said clearly upset Andrew. His mouth slashed into a frown, and his grip tightened. He turned his back to her and finished the conversation.

She had no right to feel shut out of his life but she did. The barrier she had experienced New Year's Eve seemed higher, and she was aware the man she had gotten to know over the holidays was retreating and the businessman was firmly back in place.

Andrew put the receiver in its cradle with such control that another tremor shuddered down her. She wanted to ask him what was wrong, but again the sense that she was intruding where she shouldn't was underscored by the tight expression on his face when he pivoted toward her.

"If you want, I can meet you at The Garden if you're gonna be pressed for time." She clutched the straps of her purse until her hands ached.

"No, I should be all right. I'll be there at six-thirty." He strode forward, taking her by the elbow, his features softening somewhat. "But I am pressed for time now. I need to be in the president's office in ten minutes and I still have some information I need to gather."

"I understand," she murmured, one part of her mourning a loss as though Andrew had told her he never wanted to see her again. "I look forward to seeing you Saturday."

The sound of the door closing as she left his office reinforced the feeling of being shut out of his life.

* * *

Sadie paced from one end of her living room to the other, glancing at her watch for the tenth time in three minutes. Andrew was late. It was six forty-five and—

The ringing phone startled her, and she jumped. Quickly she answered it, praying nothing had happened to him. "Hello."

"Sadie, I've been delayed," Andrew said in a whispered rush. "Hopefully I'll be able to make the dinner later. Please go to the restaurant without me."

Sadie heard some people talking in the background. "I'll save you a seat. Good—"

The phone line went dead. Sadie stood in the middle of her living room holding the receiver and listening to the dial tone. Then, as if she finally realized she was going to be late for a dinner in her honor, she hung up the phone, snatched her purse and hurried to her car, pushing her swirling emotions to the background. She didn't have time to feel—to fall apart.

Five minutes after seven, she entered The Garden and the hostess directed her to the back room where the dinner was being held. She found the table her parents were sitting at and slipped into the empty chair next to her father.

"Where's Andrew?" he asked, passing her the basket of rolls.

"He'll be late. He got tied up at work."

"At Christmas he was telling me about the demands of his job. He has a lot of responsibility at IFI."

"Yes, he does." She heard the tension in her voice and wasn't surprised at her father's probing look.

"Are you two serious?"

"We're just friends, Dad. As you said, Andrew is too busy for much of a life outside of his work."

"There's nothing wrong with a man working hard."

She was thankful the waitress started serving the main course of roasted chicken so she didn't have to reply to her father's statement. He would feel that way, since most of his life he'd buried himself in his work, often to the neglect of his family. She already felt wrung out and certainly didn't want to get into that with her father.

Every time the door opened to admit someone into the private dining room, Sadie looked, expecting to see Andrew. By the time the waitress removed the main course and brought out the dessert, Sadie gave up.

When the superintendent rose and went to the podium, her stomach twisted into a huge knot. This was a big moment, and she wanted Andrew sitting next to her. Her father reached over and took her hand, squeezing it as the man spoke about the honor of being selecting as a teacher of the year from a school. Then the superintendent described each candidate up for teacher of the year from the Cimarron City public schools.

"Our candidate representing the high school has many roles as a teacher of special needs students. Within her classroom she has faced many challenges that most would never dream of dealing with. She has gone beyond her role as a special education teacher to set up a peer tutoring program for regular education students at Cimarron High School. It is heartwarming to see these peer tutors forming friendships and helping with students who have special needs. Outside the classroom she is a coach for Special Olympics and enjoys taking her team to many sports activities throughout the year. She also is the vocational coordinator, visiting job sites where her students work as well as developing potential job sites for possible employment opportunities for her students. Please give a round of applause for Sadie Spencer.''

Blushing, Sadie stood. She was never comfortable with compliments. After she resumed her seat, the superintendent went through the rest of the candidates.

"Each one of these teachers would be a great representative for our school district. Now I have the good fortune to announce..." He paused and tore open an envelope.

Sadie's mother leaned in front of her father and whispered, "I feel like I'm at the Academy Awards. Good luck, sweetheart."

"She's the best. She doesn't need luck," her father said. "If she doesn't win, it's their loss."

Sadie's gaze fastened onto her father.

"The winner is Sadie Spencer from Cimarron High School."

"I knew you would win." Her father winked at her.

She sat in her chair, speechless, not having prepared anything to say. She heard the applause, but the sound seemed far away.

Her father nudged her gently in the side. "You'd better go up to the podium."

"I didn't write a speech."

"You'll think of something. It's rare that you don't have something to say."

On the long walk to the front of the room the one thing that kept repeating itself in her mind was how much she wished Andrew was here to share her good news. She glanced at the door one last time before stepping up to the podium.

"I'm speechless," she said into the mike.

"We know better than that, Sadie. You're never speechless," a fellow high school teacher called.

Sadie smiled. "What I meant is that I didn't write a speech. The other candidates were so deserving that I didn't allow myself to think about winning this honor, and indeed it is an honor to represent this school district for Oklahoma Teacher of the Year. Cimarron public schools are simply the best in the state."

Applause erupted, and a few cheers.

Sadie waited until the noise died down to continue. "I have a lot of people to thank for me being here tonight, but without God's guidance and support I wouldn't be standing here receiving this honor. He is the first one I must thank. The next are the students I'm privileged to teach. I have learned so much from them and hopefully in the process have taught them some life lessons. Then, of course, I must include in this list my parents and the staff I work with at Cimarron High School. Thank you.''

Amidst clapping and a standing ovation, Sadie took the plaque from the superintendent and shook his hand. She started to walk to her chair when he stopped her.

Leaning into the microphone, the superintendent said, ''That speech is one of the many reasons we chose Sadie Spencer for this honor. She will represent our school district well at the state level. Thank you, Sadie, for teaching our children.''

Sadie made her way toward her table, pausing to shake people's hands and to exchange a few words with some people she'd taught with for years. When she arrived at her chair, her father rose and hugged her, then her mother. Tears welled in Sadie's eyes. Her father rarely embraced her, and certainly not in front of so many people. This should be one of the happiest moments of her life, and yet there was a part of her that was sad, as though the evening wasn't totally complete without Andrew. When had she come to depend on him to define her happiness?

''Honey, you were wonderful up there,'' her mother said, kissing her on the cheek. ''Don't you think so, Robert?''

''You couldn't have prepared a better speech, if you ask me.'' Pride oozed from his voice. ''You really enjoy teaching your students, don't you?''

''Yes, Dad, very much.'' Peering into his eyes, she finally saw understanding about her choice to become a teacher for students with special needs.

"I guess I never stopped to really listen to you."

Tears cascaded down her cheeks. She wiped them away, only to have more replace them.

"After this is over, we need to celebrate. Where would you like to go, Sadie?" her father asked, his arm around her shoulders.

"Home." She needed to leave before she totally broke down in front of everyone.

"We can do that. I believe your mom baked a cake this afternoon for the occasion."

It took Sadie twenty minutes to make it to her car. She hoped she murmured the right words to everyone's congratulations, but she wasn't sure. She felt confused, at loose ends, when she should be flying high. The realization of how important Andrew was to her, someone who had prided herself on her independence, distressed her.

She followed her parents to their house and pulled in behind them in the driveway, upset that even as she'd weaved her way through the crowd at the restaurant, she had kept looking for Andrew to appear. By the time she entered her parents' home, anger at being stood up tangled with her worry that something had happened to Andrew.

"I need to make a phone call." Sadie sought the privacy of her father's office.

She dialed Andrew's office, but there was no answer. She called his house and got his answering machine. Her worry mushroomed. She decided to check her messages to make sure he hadn't left one.

"Sadie, I'm sorry I can't make it to the dinner after

all. There's a problem I need to see to personally in Seattle. I'm leaving tonight. I'll call you when I get back.''

The aloofness in his voice chilled Sadie. She hung up but remained sitting at her father's desk, immersed in conflicting emotions. She knew he had warned her about what was happening. His work came first and always would. He hadn't promised her a thing, and yet she had secretly hoped for more. And now she would pay for it. Her heart broke, the deep ache making each breath difficult.

The tears flowed unchecked down her face as she leaned back in the overstuffed chair and closed her eyes.

''Sadie? What's wrong?''

Surprised to hear her father's voice, she bolted up, her eyes snapping open. ''I—I—'' She couldn't find the words to explain the anguish she felt.

''What happened? Something with Andrew?''

The concern in her father's voice unleashed more tears. His image shimmered as he strode to her and reclined against the desk, his hands gripping its edge.

She sucked in a gulp of air. ''Andrew's okay.''

Her father remained quiet, waiting for her to continue.

''Daddy, I'll always be alone.'' Fresh tears burned her eyes as she spoke for the first time her biggest fear. She had pushed people away because she was afraid they would do it first. Andrew and she were alike in that respect.

''No, you won't.'' He clasped her arms and drew

her to her feet. "You will always have me and your mother. I know that I haven't been the best dad in the world, but I do love you."

With her head against his shoulder, she remembered Andrew's encouragement to talk with her father about how she felt growing up. She swallowed hard, but her throat was still tight and dry.

"Dad, I'd like to talk to you about something." Her voice was raspy.

"What about?"

She pulled back. "Not being perfect," she blurted, her breath bottled in her lungs.

His brow wrinkled. "I know you aren't perfect. No one is."

"But you were never satisfied with my accomplishments. You always wanted me to do better."

"Of course, I wanted you to do better. I want the best for my daughter, but that didn't mean I wasn't proud of you."

"What if I don't get Oklahoma Teacher of the Year? How will you feel?"

He looked as though she'd punched him in the stomach. "You don't think I would be proud of you anymore if you don't win the next level?"

She nodded.

"You couldn't be more wrong, Sadie. I'll be disappointed that the committee couldn't see you're the best in the state, but I'll still be proud of you. I—" Her father's eyes grew round. He twisted away and began to pace, plowing his fingers through his hair. "I never said it, did I?"

"No."

He stopped and faced her. "I'm sorry."

Never once in his life had her father told her he was sorry. Her throat closed, emotions buried for years surfacing.

"Your mom says that's something I need to work on. I've made quite a few mistakes with this family. Reverend Littleton is helping me to see that I shut down after your little brother died. I turned away from your mother, from you. I never properly grieved his death."

"Oh, Daddy." Sadie rushed to her father and hugged him.

He held her tight. "I've caused you a lot of tears, haven't I? I hope you can forgive me."

"We're family." His comfort soothed her troubled soul. She knew they still had a long way to go in developing the kind of father-daughter relationship she dreamed about, but this evening was a start.

"Am I the reason you're crying right now?"

"No." She could hear his heart pounding and drew strength from him. "I wish Andrew could have come tonight."

"What happened to him?"

"Business called him away from Cimarron City."

"I'm sorry about that, Sadie, but with a man like Andrew, who is dedicated to his work, that kind of thing will happen. You have to learn to accept that."

It might have been possible for her to accept his work schedule, but Andrew wasn't giving her a chance. He was pulling away. She had heard it in his voice. She needed to protect herself before there was nothing left to protect.

A pile of papers sat on Andrew's lap, but all he could seem to do was stare out the airplane window at the dark night—and see Sadie's face when she heard her message from him. On the ride to the airport he could have gone by the restaurant and talked with her personally instead of taking the easy way out. But he'd been afraid if he had seen her disappointment he would have stayed, and he couldn't. He was the one at IFI who was supposed to get the negotiations with the union back on track.

He rubbed a hand down his face, wishing he could scrub away the disgust he felt toward himself. He hadn't wanted to hurt Sadie, but he knew he had. He had warned her he wasn't a settling-down kind of guy—but for a while there he had pictured himself with Sadie as his wife, living in a house with a white picket fence, a dog and children. These past few weeks, since the New Year, he was reminded of the type of work schedule he had. There was no room in it for a wife and family. The only decent thing left for him to do was end it with Sadie.

His chest hurt with the thought. But he was no good at relationships and long ago he had stopped dreaming about having a family. Work didn't demand an emotional commitment, people did.

This time last week Sadie had been summoned to Mrs. Lawson's office because there was a problem with Chris. Now she stood in the middle of IFI's large lobby, undecided whether to see Mrs. Lawson first, or Andrew. She peered at the doors that led into the mail room. Business first. While the reason she was here to see Andrew was certainly not pleasure, it was personal.

With determined steps she covered the distance to the mail room and thrust open the door. Sadie waved to Chris as she headed for Mrs. Lawson's office. After one sharp rap the woman admitted Sadie.

"I won't keep you long, but I was in the building and wanted to check on Chris and the problem we discussed last week. Are things better?" Sadie remained by the door.

"Chris seems to be conducting himself properly."

"Are there any other problems I should know about?"

Mrs. Lawson shook her head. "He's eager to learn and works hard while he is here."

Surprised at the softening in the older woman's features, Sadie relaxed her taut body and smiled. "I'm glad he's working out."

Mrs. Lawson returned her smile. "Yes, better than I thought when Mr. Knight approached me about this program."

Sadie turned toward the door, glanced back and said, "Thank you, Mrs. Lawson. If you have any other problems concerning Chris, please free feel to call me."

Sadie briefly spoke to Chris before leaving the mail room. Her gaze slid from the glass doors that led outside to the bank of elevators. She knew that Andrew had returned home sometime yesterday because he had left her a message on her answering machine, congratulating her on becoming the teacher of the year. Nothing else was said, and the silence after his message had been deafening.

What to do? Andrew was a friend, and when she was in a building where a friend worked she always stopped by to say hello. Her rationalization worked for all of one minute, but she knew by the time she had punched the button for his floor that she really wanted to see him to put an end to this roller coaster ride she had felt herself on these past few months.

"Hold the elevator," a woman called.

Sadie pressed her finger on the open door button. Jollie stepped onto the elevator, surprise evident in her expression.

"So the rumors are true," the other woman said.

"What rumors?" Sadie asked, knowing what Jollie was going to say.

"That you and Andrew Knight are an item. Is he another bachelor we're gonna lose for next year?"

"We are friends. He's safe," Sadie said, realizing she would probably have to get used to that idea, except that she didn't think she could be Andrew's friend. Being around him and not showing her love would be too much for her to handle. She wore her emotions on her face, and she wasn't that good an actress.

"Then why are you here?"

"I have a student working here."

"Yes, I heard, in the mail room. In fact, Chris comes into my office every day. What a breath of sunshine. All the employees like him and look forward to his afternoon visit."

Sadie responded to the woman's words with a smile, glad that something was going right. "He likes working here."

"I'm going to have an opening in my department soon. Would Chris be interested in working in receiving?"

"I'll talk with him about it."

"He'll have to apply, but I hope he does. I know how difficult Mrs. Lawson can be to work for, and if Chris is doing okay for her, he'll be an asset for my department."

"I'll get with Andrew about it."

"Great. See you at our first organizational meeting for the auction." The elevator doors slid open, and Jollie left.

The next floor was Andrew's, and Sadie quickly exited the elevator. She couldn't believe her good fortune when she saw that Mrs. Fox was away from her desk. Without debating, she went to Andrew's door and knocked, entering his office when she heard him say, "Come in."

Andrew glanced up from a pile of papers he was reading. Surprise quickly followed by joy flitted across his features, only to have a neutral expression descend by the time she'd crossed the office.

"How did you get past Mrs. Fox?"

"Easy. She wasn't out there. How was your trip? Successful?"

"Yes, the negotiations are back on track and should be wrapped up in a few days."

"I'm glad."

Silence fell between them, thick and heavy like a sudden summer storm. Sadie sat before her legs gave out on her. The width of his desk separated them, but she felt as if they were worlds apart. She searched for the right words to say, but his unreadable look wiped all thoughts from her mind.

"Andrew, I find being direct the best way to go through life," she began, her mouth parched as though she had stuffed wads of cotton in it.

"I find that a good philosophy."

"Then I think we should talk about us."

"Us?"

Her gaze coupled with his. "You and I both know there is an us, or there was until just recently."

Andrew surged to his feet. "Yes. We do need to talk." He strode to the large picture window that afforded him a wonderful view of Cimarron City. "I told you from the beginning I had no time for a relationship, that my life would be tied up with my work. That hasn't changed, Sadie."

His back was to her, and she needed to see what was in his eyes. She walked to him and leaned against the windowsill, fingertips digging into the ledge. "So what was December all about?"

"It was a lull in my busy schedule because of the holidays. Even IFI slows down at that time of year."

He ran his hand through his hair, then rubbed the back of his neck. "I don't want to disappoint you again like I did Saturday night."

"I see."

"Do you? Do you really see?"

"Yes, I do. You're afraid to make a commitment. I believe you use your work as an excuse to justify to yourself that you have no time for anyone in your life. That's easier than risking getting hurt in a relationship."

"You have it all figured out."

"No, far from it, but I do know one thing. I'm not perfect. I have faults, and that's okay. I used to think it wasn't, that no one could see my flaws and still like me. These past few months I've come to realize differently. I have to be with a man who will commit to me one hundred percent. You can't do that, and I think you're right that we should end whatever we had between us."

Andrew straightened, quickly scrambling to conceal the anger that flashed in his eyes. "Good. Then we agree."

Sadie started for the door, determined to remain in control. "Oh, by the way, Jollie wants Chris to apply for a position in the receiving department when it opens up."

"I'll look into it." His reply was cold.

At the door she paused and said, "I'm gonna ask you again. Have you thought about what you'll have in, say, ten or twenty years? Will it be enough to satisfy you? What happens when you retire and there is no more work?''

With those questions spoken, Sadie slipped out of the office, feeling Andrew's penetrating stare shimmer down her back. She had to go back to school for a meeting. *Please, Lord, give me the strength to make it through the rest of the day without falling apart.* She uttered the prayer over and over as she felt her heart shatter into a thousand pieces.

Chapter Thirteen

Andrew started to knock, hesitated and dropped his arm to his side. Turning away, he walked a few paces down the hall, then stopped and twisted, staring at the door. When Sadie had left his office the day before yesterday, he'd felt as though she had sucked the air from the room and taken it with her. Her questions still rang in his mind, demanding answers he didn't have. He needed help and had run out of places to go.

The door opened, and Reverend Littleton appeared in the hallway. "Andrew? What brings you to the church?"

Andrew stared at the man, two nights without sleep dulling his mind. He couldn't get Sadie out of his thoughts, especially the devastation he'd glimpsed in her eyes that last time he'd seen her in his office.

"What's wrong, my son?"

Andrew flinched. He could remember Tom saying

those very words to him when he'd first lived with Tom. Over the two years he'd lived with Tom, he'd learned to put his trust and faith in the man and the Lord. Then Tom had been taken away just as quickly and disastrously as his family, and he'd felt himself floundering for a safety net.

Tunneling his fingers through his tousled hair, Andrew approached the reverend. "I need your help."

Reverend Littleton stepped to the side. "Come into my office and let's talk."

Seated in a comfortable chair across from the older man, Andrew closed his eyes for a moment, gathering his scattered thoughts into a coherent pattern. Finally, at four in the morning, he had come to the conclusion he needed more in his life than what he had. Sadie was right. There was nothing there that would mean anything in the years to come.

Andrew took a deep, cleansing breath. "How do you find your way back to God?"

"Son, I think you've taken the first step today by coming here and asking that question."

"This is an unexpected visit, Andrew. Is something wrong with the union negotiations?"

Andrew remained standing in front of Mr. Wilson's desk. "No, I've come to withdraw my name from consideration for the presidency of IFI."

"May I ask why?"

"My goals and plans for the future have changed these past few months."

"They still involve IFI?"

"Yes, but not as its president. I want to start a family."

Surprise flitted across Mr. Wilson's features. "Are congratulations in order?"

"I haven't convinced the lady yet."

"If I know you, Andrew, that's only a technicality. Who do you like as the next president?"

Andrew pulled up a chair and sat, more relaxed now that he had told Mr. Wilson his wish. "Charles would be excellent."

"Would you be willing to take on a different role at IFI?"

"What?" Andrew asked, wary that he would be trading one all-consuming job for another.

"I want to divide your job and expand the special projects part. With you heading that section, someone else can oversee the human resource department. I like this project you're doing with Cimarron High School and their vocational program. Connected to this position, of course, would be community awareness of IFI here in Cimarron City as well as globally. Image in today's market is everything. What do you think?"

Andrew shifted, leaning forward, enthusiasm building inside him. "I like it. Tell me more."

The hairs on the nape of Sadie's neck tingled. She scanned the gym at the University of Oklahoma, her gaze skipping from Special Olympics participant to coach to spectator. She saw familiar people, but no one staring at her. Still, the sensation someone was looking at her plagued her as she walked with her team toward the court they would play on.

She placed her gym bag on the floor. "Let's stretch and warm up first."

The eight team members formed a circle. Chris went into the middle and demonstrated one stretch. Everyone followed his lead. Sadie bent over and touched the floor along with her players. As she straightened, again the feeling someone was staring at her inundated her. She looked from side to side. When she glanced behind her, she saw him.

Andrew smiled at her, nodding his head in greeting.

Shock swept through her. Andrew was dressed in gym shorts and a T-shirt with a whistle around his neck. He would be their referee. Her shock quickly turned to confusion. Why wasn't he working? Just because it was Saturday didn't mean it was a day off for him. He had no days off.

Ignoring his heartwarming smile, she focused her attention on the stretches her students were performing. But each time she lunged, reached or twisted, she couldn't shake the prickly sensation Andrew was following every move she made.

Halfway through the exercises, she slipped away from the circle to confront the man. She marched up to him, fisted her hands on her waist and demanded, "Why are you here?"

"I'm volunteering."

"Don't you have work to do or something?" She winced at the panic in her voice and wished he hadn't heard it. She knew he had. A gleam entered his eyes.

"No. I took the weekend off."

"Why?"

"To volunteer at the Winter Games for Special Olympics. I thought that was obvious."

"Nothing about you is obvious. Are you refereeing our game?"

He nodded.

"Then I'm gonna protest."

"Why?"

"I'm sure this is a conflict of interest."

"You don't think I can be fair-minded?"

"I—" She suppressed her retort. "Yes, I guess so."

"Besides, all the other referees are busy, and they're shorthanded as it is. I thought you would be happy to see me. You're the one who convinced me that Special Olympics is a good cause to donate my time to."

She narrowed her eyes, wishing they could pierce his thick skin. He was enjoying her discomfort at his presence. "You could have volunteered for one of the other sports being played at the winter games."

"But I know how to play basketball. I thought that was important if I was gonna referee." He peered over her shoulder at her team. "They have five more minutes before the game starts. I need the captain to call the coin toss."

"I'll send Chris over." Sadie marched to the circle of players, aware of Andrew's gaze assessing her, and told Chris to meet with Andrew.

Chris's face lit with a bright smile. "Mr. Knight is our referee?"

"Yes."

"That's great. He'll get to see me play. I told him about this."

So that was how Andrew knew about the winter games. Sadie wanted to discover just how much Chris and Andrew had talked about this weekend. Did Andrew mention her? Why was he here? As her thoughts began to run rampant with all the possibilities, she put a halt to the questions. Showing up for one day didn't mean anything. Special Olympics was a great cause, and she was tickled pink Andrew was giving his time to something other than work. But that was all. One day isn't a lifetime commitment, she reminded herself as she prepared her team for the start.

The game was excruciatingly slow. The seconds dragged into minutes, and Sadie could hardly keep her mind on her team. Her gaze kept returning to Andrew in the middle of her students, looking as though he was enjoying himself. He appeared relaxed, the tense lines in his face gone.

"Spencer, in?" Donnie tapped her on the shoulder and pointed toward the court.

"Okay, but remember that goal is the Chargers'. Don't shoot at that basket," Sadie said, waving toward a hoop.

The score was tied eight to eight with their opponents getting some help from Donnie, who had made a basket for the Chargers. When Donnie ran onto the

court, Sadie shouted, "Remember this is our goal."
She pointed to the north end again.

In Donnie's excitement at getting another chance
to play, he rebounded the ball and immediately took
a shot at the Chargers' goal. The ball circled the rim
and dropped through the net. Moaning, Sadie buried
her face in her hands while their opponents exploded
with applause. She thought of taking Donnie out and
decided not to. He loved to shoot baskets and was
quite good. Maybe he could make a few for them,
too.

Two minutes later, the score was eleven to ten in
the Chargers' favor. Andrew blew the whistle, announcing the end of the game. Donnie went up for a
shot and made yet another basket for the Chargers.
Thankfully this one didn't count. The team shuffled
off the court, their heads hanging. Donnie still stood
at the basket, rebounding and shooting.

"Coach, we should have won," Chris said, throw-
ing a narrow-eyed look toward Donnie.

"Everyone gets to play. You know that, even Donnie. He made five of our baskets."

"Yeah, and seven for them."

"Did you enjoy playing?"

"Yes."

"Then that's all that counts. We're here to have
fun and make new friends. Now, we have some time
before our next game. Why don't you get some water
and rest?"

"Can I have my face painted?"

"We'll do that later."

"Good. I want Sooners here." Chris pointed to his left cheek. "And Cowboys here." He gestured to the other side of his face.

Sadie laughed, tousling his hair. "Covering all your bases," she said in reference to the two big universities in the state. Chris was a huge fan of both.

Sadie returned to the court to retrieve Donnie before the next teams played. He didn't want to leave. Andrew came up behind Sadie and caught the ball as it bounced off the rim. Donnie frowned at him.

"Sorry, buddy. The next game is gonna start soon. You can shoot some baskets later."

Donnie stared at the ball clutched in Andrew's grasp, then stomped off to sit on the sideline. Sadie started to follow her student.

"I'm not refereeing this next game. I have a break. Can we talk?"

His question halted her progress toward the sideline. She didn't turn and face him. She didn't want to look into his eyes and find her resolve to get on with her life melting. "I'd rather not. I have strategies to form. We have to win all the rest of our games to win the tournament."

"You should have no problem winning if you just leave Donnie under your goal, tell him not to move and get the ball to him. Problem solved."

She heard the snap of his fingers and whirled, her anger rising. "And your specialty is solving problems."

"Yes—except my own. I haven't done a very good job there."

She placed her fisted hands on her waist. "And what problems do you have? I thought you had your life all planned out five years in advance."

The sound of balls slapping against the floor and hitting the backboard, the cheers when a person made a basket, the murmurs of voices in the crowd filled the air. Scanning the area, Sadie saw the next teams coming onto the court her students had been playing on, but none of that mattered. Her whole being focused on Andrew several feet away.

"A big one." He shortened the distance between them. "I've made a mess of my life. I've discovered the plans I made don't fit the new me."

Her eyes widened. "The new you?"

He grasped her arm. "Can we go somewhere less public to talk?"

Again she took in her surroundings, her students sitting with their families drinking water and talking. "I can't go far. We have another game soon."

"How about outside in the corridor?"

"Andrew—"

"Please, Sadie, this is important."

The beat of her heart picked up speed. Hope began to blossom in her, and she had to stamp it down before she got hurt any more than she already was. "Fine. I can spare ten minutes."

She followed him from the gym and down the corridor until he found a less crowded area. The sound of people cheering could still be heard, but Sadie felt as though the rest of the world had disappeared with only her and Andrew left. Her emotions lay bare and exposed. But as she recalled the life he'd chosen, she shored up her defenses and faced him in the alcove.

"What is it you need to tell me?" she asked, hearing the steel thread running through her words. *Dear Lord, I have to be strong. I can't deal with another rejection.*

He drew in a deep breath, glanced away for a few seconds, then directed his look at her, an intensity in his gaze. "I was wrong. I thought I could live without you. I can't."

Sadie raised her hand to stop him from saying another word. "Don't, Andrew. You were right from the beginning. It won't work for us. We want different things from life."

"No, we don't. I'd convinced myself I didn't need anyone to make me happy. That work was a good substitute. Then you came along and forced me to examine my life. I didn't like what I saw, what I'd become. I want what Tom had taught me was important—family, God."

Tears burned in her eyes. She'd longed to hear those words ever since she'd met him. Still, years of holding her emotions inside for fear of being rejected kept her quiet.

"When Tom died so unexpectedly, in my grief and anger, I turned away from the Lord, from all that Tom had shown me. Give me a chance to prove I can make a commitment, Sadie. I love you and want to spend the rest of my life proving to you what a good husband and father I can be."

Tears streamed down her face. Emotions clogged her throat, making it impossible to say anything.

Andrew caressed her cheek with his forefinger, brushing her tears away. "I met with Mr. Wilson and withdrew my name from consideration for the presidency. I made it clear to him that my priorities have changed." His touch lingered, one hand cupping her face while the other clasped her arm to bring her closer. "Say something."

Sadie swallowed hard. "I'm afraid, Andrew. Work has driven you for years."

He brought his other hand up to frame her face. "Have faith in me, Sadie. People can change if they want it bad enough, and I want this very bad."

She inhaled then exhaled slowly. "I don't think I can do anything else. I love you, Andrew Knight. God has taught me the importance of faith and giving people second chances. Yes, I'll marry you."

A smile transformed his serious expression. He feathered his lips across hers, then deepened the kiss while winding his arms around her. "You'll learn one thing about me hasn't changed. When I set my mind to do something, I do it. We will have a good life, Sadie Spencer."

Epilogue

With her arms folded over her chest, Sadie leaned against the wall in the hotel ballroom and watched the next bachelor step onto the stage. The door opened near her. She turned to see who had entered.

"Where's that man of yours?" Jollie asked, slipping into the place next to Sadie along the back wall. "The least he could do is return to the scene of his downfall."

Sadie laughed. "I hope he doesn't see it that way." With a quick look at the door, she saw another person enter the ballroom, but that man wasn't Andrew, either. "He's late."

"He's probably at work." Jollie cocked her head to the side. "On second thought, he's usually left before me these past few months. You've definitely changed that man. I never thought I would see the day he didn't burn the midnight oil."

"How's Chris doing?"

"He's working out great. I'm glad he transferred to my department. The people love seeing him come to work. He brightens the place."

Again someone pushed the door open, and Sadie glanced toward it. A smile lit her face when she spied Andrew in the entrance to the ballroom. She waved, and he headed toward her.

Jollie leaned toward her. "I should be angry you took the most eligible bachelor off the auction block. But after all the men he persuaded to donate their time to this charity auction, I can't complain."

"Neither can I." Sadie slipped her hand in Andrew's.

"It's nice to see you, Jollie."

"I'd better get back to the table I'm manning. See you two later."

"Sorry I'm late. I got detained longer than I thought at the church with the appropriation committee meeting, then the contractor called and needed to see me about our house."

His whispered words fanned her neck in warm waves. She shivered, and he brought his hands up to pull her against him. "Is there a problem with the house?"

"Not anymore. Ready to leave?"

"Leave? I thought we were staying to eat dinner."

"Nope. I've made other plans for us. This is our first anniversary."

Sadie twisted, looking at Andrew. "We were married six months ago."

"But this is where we first met, this time last year." He took her hand and tugged her toward the door.

"Where are we going?"

"It's a surprise." He opened the car door for her. "Sit back and relax."

Sadie reflected on the past year. She hadn't thought her life could get any better. Today at the doctor's it had. Laying her hand on her stomach, she smiled. Remembering the money she'd spent at the auction the year before, she decided that was the best five hundred fifty dollars she'd ever spent.

Andrew parked his car in the driveway of a home under construction. "We're here."

"At our house?"

"Come on." Andrew unlocked the door and switched on the light.

Sadie entered the almost completed house, her heels clicking on the concrete slab. Soon the carpet and hardwood floors would be put in. Soon she and Andrew would move in.

In the middle of the living room a table set for two with a white tablecloth and candles beckoned. She crossed to the table and ran her hand over a china plate.

"You thought of everything."

"Surprised?" He came up behind her and drew her against him.

"No, not really. I'm discovering how romantic my husband can be." She turned in his loose embrace so she could face him. "It's been a wonderful year."

"It's been a life-altering year."

The warm look in his eyes, so filled with love, melted her against him. "And the life-altering part isn't over with."

A silent question entered his expression. "You went to the doctor?"

"Yes, I couldn't wait until tomorrow. You know me and surprises. He confirmed we're going to have a baby."

Andrew's shout for joy echoed through the empty house as he whirled her around.

"I take it you're happy about the baby," she said when he settled her feet on the concrete floor.

* * * * *

Dear Reader,

For many years I have worked with students with special needs. I wanted to write about the students I am fortunate to work with each day. I wanted to show what a wonderful gift these students are to society. They have hopes and dreams like everyone else. They enjoy working and they enjoy playing sports. I have coached Special Olympics for years and think this organization is a worthy one. I have gotten such joy from seeing one of my students participate in a sport, and whether he wins or not, doesn't matter. You can volunteer with Special Olympics in your state. They can always use a person to congratulate an athlete when he has crossed the finish line whether he is first or last.

I hope you enjoy Sadie and Andrew's story and the blessings a student with special needs can bring to a person. Again I want to thank God for giving me the chance to teach students with such a zeal for life and an unconditional love for others. I love hearing from readers. You may write me at P.O. Box 2074, Tulsa, OK 74101.

May God bless you,

Margaret Daley

Next Month From Steeple Hill®'s

Love Inspired®

Love at Last
by
Irene Brand

On a business trip, media consultant Lorene Harvey
accidentally meets her college sweetheart, Perry Saunders.
Even after twenty years, they still have feelings for each
other. But Lorene has a secret two decades old that she
fears Perry will never forgive. Will she be able to put her
trust in faith and find the strength needed to find
Perry's love and forgiveness?

**Don't miss
LOVE AT LAST**

On sale November 2002

LILAL

Next Month From Steeple Hill's

Love Inspired

A Time To Forgive
by
Marta Perry

When Adam Caldwell commissioned artist Tory Marlowe
to design a stained-glass window for the local church,
the last thing he expected was to be reunited with this
mysterious woman he'd met one magical night fifteen
years ago. Like Cinderella, she'd disappeared from his
life at the stroke of midnight. But when Tory's arrival
threatens to expose a long-hidden secret, will Adam let
his pride get in the way of a love finally found…?

Don't miss
A TIME TO FORGIVE

On sale December 2002

Next Month From Steeple Hill's

Love Inspired

The Christmas Groom
by
Deb Kastner

In order to escape his unhappy family, Colin Brockman
enlisted in the navy while studying to be a navy
chaplain. He's finally enjoying freedom for the first
time in his life when he meets straitlaced graduate
student Holly McCade. Though they couldn't be more
different, Holly and Colin can't deny their attraction
for each other. Will this mismatched couple prove that
opposites really can make a perfect match?

Don't miss
THE CHRISTMAS GROOM

On sale December 2002